Peggy Mercer

The Traveler

Peggy Mercer

Credits

The Traveler © *Peggy Mercer, July 9, 2023.* is a novel of inspirational, Southern Fiction, Historical non-fiction, Spirituality and Literary lyrical fiction. The book is published by www.peggymercerworldwide.org, and set in coastal, middle, and north Georgia. It is printed in the U.S.A. and protected by worldwide copyright laws, Pan American and International copyrights.

The book is available at Amazon and in Kindle format for electronic readers, Wal Mart Books online, bookstores and in foreign countries.

No part of this book can be used without permission of the author.

Cover art from a painting by Bart Mills, Colorado.

References to the song, *I Want to Stroll Over Heaven with You,* by permission of family of "Mountain Man Carl" Trivette, written at age 17 (1952) as a love song to Marilee Rasnake Trivette.

References to the *Oak Ridge Boys* by habit.

Dedication

This book is dedicated to the precious memory of the following fur-babies:

Rocket to the Moon (Peggy Mercer), *Maci – Come on Baby* (Kenneth and Janice Smith), *Daisy* (Ronda McNeil Sports), *Roxie* (Lucy Taylor), *Moonshine* (Erik and Lisa Cobb, Katie Paul, and Frank Harrell),
and
Ruffy (Judy McConnell), *Finn* and *Willow* (Debra Childers and Sierra Childers), *Big Guy* (Rhonda Sylvester Meeks), *Tess* (Kawana V. Whittle), *Willy* (Connie King Corbi and Michael Corbi), *Silas* (Brooke and Tracy Bennett),
And
Duke (Brenda Finch), *Sugarbear* (Howard Kennedy), *Snickers* (John and Linda Oemler), *Jack* (Nan Kirkland), Harley (Kim Jowers).

Author's Note and Acknowledgements

Shortly after I started *The Traveler*, (Book three in the Big Daddy Island stories) I went through a year of disastrous health, which prevented me from writing for long periods of time. Thanks everyone who prayed for me because the prayers worked miracles, and I am writing again!

I especially thank John Richards, who was there in coastal Georgia when I went through surgery (twice) and brought me home. Thanks to Hilton Markette, a retired U.S. Marshal for his valuable input and to Animal Control officer, Tim Gay, for his input. Thanks to Tim Morris, Allen Field, and Rhonda Meeks, who always have my back.

Thanks, with all my heart to my best friend, Brenda Finch, who gave me permission (and constant encouragement) to write three novels and a ton of poetry about **Big Daddy** and his coastal Georgia "island."

The Traveler

THE TRAVELER

PROLOGUE

Some people don't believe in God, but Malikhan Sharon (pronounced Mali-can-Shay-rone) did. Malikhan, or Malik for short, believed in God, and that all living creatures, are created by our Heavenly Father. We are family, he thought, standing on the dock jutting out from the edge of Big Daddy Island. Might be foster family in a way, but still family! Every person is family, and supernaturally gifted, celestially created by the same Father in Heaven.

Some people do not believe in supernatural healing, how cellular changes occur in a body and unexplained healing occurs, but Malikhan Sharon did. When people pray, Malikhan thought, people and their precious fur babies are healed. This happens when people pray, believing! These are signs of his all power, and yes, he honors those who believe. (Bible: Signs shall follow those who believe!)

Some people don't believe how living creatures have souls, but Malik did. And how precious are God's creatures, great and small, he thought. How spiritual they are; divine.

He stood close to the North River, at the edge of the marsh, green as emeralds, peridots, jades, gold threaded stalks, loving this place and this mission he was launching at Big Daddy Island on the Georgia coast. It was his dream come true mission for which he'd been foreordained. Chosen was the word. Many are called, Malik knew, but few are chosen, like him. No brag; just facts.

He had been set apart, for many times and places and this was one of
them. This time at Big Daddy Island. This work, this project or mission. If people only

knew what I knew. If they had been with me through time, through the missions and the sights, oh my! Dear Lord, Malik thought, people think they are done for, as they get older and have no more work to do on this earth. But they are wrong. So wrong!

Malik giggled hoarsely and felt the July breeze brush his face. Big Daddy Island, so close to the ocean he could smell it, taste it, wade through (at low tide) the marsh (watching out for gators of course) and come out at the Sapelo Island workstation. He was hollering distance from the people at the

workstation around the bend. If he stuck to the edge of the marsh, he could walk around there in no time flat. Past the overhanging palm trees and oaks, festooned with Spanish moss, he could see the station. He often waved to the man working the crane with the American flag, "Old Glory" flying from the top.

He now caught the scents of shrimp and mud, snails, and the decaying, once white, rowboat, abandoned in the marsh. The rowboat was now a resting place for birds and Malik had seen a coon eating a fish, and a bobcat standing on the back of the boat gazing at something across the marsh.

There is always another mission, another job to do. God puts you where he wants you.

These are those "ordered steps" spoken of in the Bible. These are the foreordained "Plans I have for you" guides. He planned our lives before we were in our earthly mother's womb. Think about it!

We are born to earth, and until our final gasp of breath, everyone has work to do. Old or young, each phase of life brings us to the next stage. We are almost always where God wants us to be, at whatever point on our earthly journey. Our purpose is to be there!

He orchestrates as we carry out our plans, and get the results bestowed upon our life. Spread God's great love, shower others who might be in the "dark" with the light of God's love. Through the work before us, at each phase of life, our purpose is to make marks.

You might be called on to be a singing star, if so, sing one for Jesus (or more). You might be called on to write, if so, lift him up, because the "Gospel" so prophesied, must be published to every living creature and all mankind before the second coming. It is our work. Although we might not want to do yet another job, another project, do we have a choice?

God calls us and we hear His voice, and we know the voice and He is the parent, and we are the children, so we ask "Yes, sir?"

We must of course, make sure God is the one calling us and not us calling us. Some people get excited about a project and call it a "call" from God or "wherever God is leading me…" and then find out it wasn't God calling. It was us caught up in a great idea. Then we are back to square one. Waiting on God's call again. Like winds to and fro, woe!

Malik, however, knew when God was calling. He had heard the voice before, many times. He knew when the Master called.

So be it. "My sheep will know my voice…" thought Malik and felt the power within him urging him forward to this mission, to make a deep and lasting, loving mark on mankind!

He wanted to remember he heard the voice of our Father in Heaven, saying to him, you are in this life for a reason. You have purpose, you are needed: go forth.

Don't worry about age, skin color, strengths or weaknesses, just step one foot forward and I will carry you the rest of the way. "Go on Malik, in Jesus's name!"

Peggy Mercer

Chapter 1:
Send Me

"Take a break from life," said the earthly man within Malik. "Go on vacation, rest up, eat, drink and be merry for a while. You deserve a time out!" The earthly man giggled silly.

"Oh my, and no," said Malikhan Sharon. "Don't stop now; never quit! Over the next hill: home and a lot of time on your hands!"

"But you are too old. Your new calling needs time, and it's short, okay? And energy, you'll need energy, and it's mostly gone!" said the earthly man.

"Oh my, and no," said Malik,

"Only your Father in Heaven knows when your clock moves forward no more."

Both the spirit man and the earthly man lived within Malikhan Sharon. Both debated every thought, every idea, but because we souls will not go gentle into the long night, because we don't want to stop and take time out, because we work our entire lives to build our houses of stuff and get great things done on the side, we don't want to give time the time it needs to rest.

Within Malik, the spirit man always won. As within so many of us, so it was with Malik. We all feel led at times! Malik heard the call and felt led.

Even as the world says we are too old for final callings upon our lives, our spirits guide us along His paths, laid out like yellow brick roads before us. As Malik gazed at the green marsh, miles and miles of beauty, the scripture came to him: "For I know the plans I have for you," declares the Lord, "plans to prosper you and not to harm you, plans to give you hope and a future." Jeremiah, 29:11.

Malik felt the fire--always present in a work for God—leap within him and he was consumed by a fire of excitement. Nothing he'd experienced or gone through, no world event, no shaking earth, no sun blacked out, no blood moons, no booms of thunder nor storms at sea had prepared him for this last mission. As hearts go, as souls know, this was it. He knew it surely as a star knows light.

This was it.

A man knows, by the measurements of time and place, age, past work, about when the hands of the clock must stop ticking. An educated guess rings true to the miles or lack of road ahead. He knows. He can see. Reality calls for common sense and although Malik knew he was old (hair silver, knees weak, feet hurt, back aches) he also knew
how the spirit man within him oversaw his choices. As in his every experience, if God said go, then Malik went. He answered when God called.

Malik had dreamed of this his whole life. He had dreamed of being here, starting out. He had plotted and planned. He was eager.

This was his love mission. This was his free choice. God is all about free choice. He is all about choosing the route we take to get back to Him. The going home trip.

And here on the edge of Big Daddy Island, a place Malik loved the man within his earthly temple, the friend of the earthly man, was ready to rock and roll. He couldn't wait to get started. He could not wait to see what he could and would do, guided by God, spreading that love with his every step.

Our strength may be pretty much gone, our mind blank as a desert, hands feeble, but work we must. Never stop! When God calls our name, we must shout to the mountains, and shout to the Heavens, "Send me, oh Lord, send me!"

And add, "make it quick" and then hit the ground running to see the work come forth with fruit. True work for God bears fruit.

Now, I'm back, he smiled. Back to Big Daddy Island, standing here in the glow of a rising sun, thinking about this mission. The mission of an old man who had been here before. And would go forth because over the miles upon miles of his journeys, he had found his dream.

Tears fell from his brown eyes and his hands shook, so overcome was he with emotion. The love he felt for this place, throughout the many missions, throughout the swirling of lives and places and times, Big Daddy Island had always been his happy place. He loved it here. So happy!

I am the Traveler, he thought, and I've come home for the last time. I have lived my lives, finished work before me many times, and once I found this island on the Georgia coast--realized it was paradise on earth, I've been itching to come home. Always trying to get home.

The other missions throughout my story (stories) were ordained and foreordained. I completed them as a chosen one. When I came here before I was a young married man, flirting with life, imperfect but good things going on no less. I was always the good son to my earthly mama and always the good husband and father. On that, I found happiness.

A bird squawked from the oaks to the right of the wooden dock. Malik thought about the stones inside a tiny suede pouch in his jeans pocket. He went nowhere without his precious stones. He carried 12 stones and why?

Taken from the Lord's book, 12 tribes of Israel and 12 stones in Aaron's breastplate and many other times when the number 12 commanded significance. God our Father loved the number 12.

He still loves it! Those who are alienated from all things spiritual will know this some fine day!

In this world, some would call him a rockhound. He loved stones and their meaning, gemstones, crystals, and their energy and purpose in life. So many people did not have a clue, buddy!

He took the small pouch from his pocket and shook the stones out into his big hand. In the palm of his big right hand were yellow jasper, (protection of his Spirituality) a small moonstone, (Symbol of new beginnings) and others which Malik would study over and share.

He wore a precious Jade shaped in a tear drop on a silver chain around his neck. Jade for protection in the journey because Malik was known as the Traveler.

What? He thought, there are people who do not understand the power of stones. BUT Malik did. Had he not seen how the 12 Tribes of Israel were represented by Twelve gemstones? Those twelve powerful stones were set in the breastplate of Aaron, the first high Priest among the Hebrews.

Among Christians, the twelve stones represented the Twelve Apostles. There is always more to a story than meets the eye, Malik thought, and put the stones back into the pouch, enjoying caressing the Jade around his neck on the silver chain.

Amazing how many journeys the jade stone had had been worn on the chain around his neck. Jade was his protecting stone and the Super-stone of Healing. Jades fills a person with an ability to express the light within. Jade allows us to harness the light within. Malik believed it filled him with the light of God which was within him. The light is within each of us. It is our power source!

You do know that your power to be, rise and excel, empower others, and spread the great love of God, is WITHIN you, the force is within you?

Malik felt high as the Georgia blue skies, thinking such, began walking along the dock back across the path leading to the island cabin, which was painted yellow, and thus "Yellow."

The Traveler

He was surrounded by Palm trees and banana trees around the cottages, and ancient oaks. Some Yaupon trees. At least 300 species of birds flew about. Snails and mud creatures crawled, jumped, sprinted throughout and above the endless fields of marsh, emerald and jade and peridot, shot with gold stalks. Paradise.

This was where he stayed. The mission plans were laid from this basecamp. Beautiful, beautiful, quiet, and peaceful for thinking things through. Especially this mission since it has to do with loving nature, animals and spreading healing and love.

Memories of another time, long ago, a few years for sure. If Malik could get off the beaten path of a certain journey, he mostly detoured here for a spell to regroup and chill.

Even Travelers need time to relax. He was tired but he was here to plan this final act of God.

Malikhan Sharon had brought few things. As a wanderer, a Traveler, he packed lightly, very lightly. He wore the same clothes, ate the same simple foods, and minimized everything.

He needed nothing. His clothing fit in with the locals whom he knew many from other side trips here, lives intertwined with former times. He knew people by name. They knew him.

He didn't stay in one place long. Drifters omen, such as him, never put down roots. His roots were in glory and glory had sent him here and would see him through.

Earthly answers must be formed and handed and banded about because Malik was able to move around, unhindered. He had abilities!

Life is full of hinderances, as we all know. He had to stay safe from the naysayers and those who would harm him and destroy his purpose!

You may entertain a big dream, and you will see nothing goes smoothly. See what happens. In the words of Malik's mama, It's always something. If we try to walk a mile in someone else's footsteps, we see fast where it goes. All roads do not go in the same direction!

Role play. Go. Do. Watch!

We set out to do something great and when rain starts falling people who don't understand become angry. Life pounds you with lemons. Things get in the way. Watch and be ready! Prepare ye!

And like lines from an old gospel song some locals often sang at the African church beside the main road, Malik hummed his version of this line, "I will always and forever, rise."

And thought of the next line, "No power on earth can ever, ever hold me back, hold me down."

He smiled and his pulse pounded. He lifted his eyes to the Georgia blue skies, reminding him of blue eyes and unconditional love and he said to the veil, "I will go where you send me, Father in Heaven."

Peggy Mercer

He closed his old eyes and thought,

I am the Traveler.

The man with wings.

Worlds without end.

CHAPTER 2:

IF IT CAN GO WRONG

Malik reached the door to Yellow and about the same time, a black SUV with a thick chrome grill swung into the path at the wooden gate, into the drive at Big Daddy Island and two men in suits emerged from the vehicle. FBI? Georgia GBI?

He could not remember what color cars were driven by whom! Black or white, who?

BUT they were here, for sure, and Malik disappeared into Yellow and grabbed a writing pad and came back out with a baseball cap on backwards. Nothing showed but silver sideburns. He smiled and was ready to talk. He could not wait to dispel their fears.

Malik sat down in a rocking chair on the long porch. The men approached, wearing stern looks with their wrinkled suits. One flashed a badge. A U.S. Marshal no less. Malik nodded and invited them to sit down. He was impressed.

"We'll stand," said the tallest man. "I am U.S. Marshal Joe Dimarks, (and Malik smiled and thought he said Dimaggio) because his hearing wasn't what it used to be, and they could see his hair was white as Georgia cotton. Beware of old men, he smiled already.

Old. Malik had moved forward through time so much for years, eons, legendary and historical events, had witnessed the world stand still a time or ten, so yes, he was old and tired. Hair white as the driven snow with a silver glow. One more mission, just one more mile had been his plea for so long and here he was.

Now what? Another interruption to deal with, he almost giggled. But no, focus on the task at hand, always an uppermost thought.

"Welcome and can I answer questions for you?" Malik asked, rocking; oh, he loved a good wood rocking chair. He was not nervous, no need to be. He had been chased around a lot in his lives and for goodness sakes, these men had no clues at all. This was just an interview of two young law enforcement agents of some breed and department and He, Malik, looked at it as small talk. Something to get through. Speed bump.

"Sure," said the shorter agent. "We are looking for a stranger in the area who may be trespassing and might be looking to harm the coast!"

"Well, it's not me," he giggled. It was hoarse, a stutter, and said, "I am a peacemaker, and my earthly name, er, my name is Malikhan Sharon,"

Mailk laughed. "Pronounced SHAY-RONE. The coast? Me? I would never harm anything!"

"From where?" Dimarks asked. He crossed his arms. "Where are you from?" Louder.

"Actually, I'm from Savannah, Georgia, and getting ready to go back up there," said Malik. "I've got to work on my tan. At my age, don't want my skin to get too dead looking," he laughed, and they didn't.

'I'm already wrinkled," Malik laughed again, and thought that was funny. They didn't.

"We are checking out strangers and looking at ID's just in case," said Dimarks. "How long have you been in the states?"

"Forever, it feels like, 70 years! I love it here. I stay here when I'm in the area. I come down here to fish out of the ocean. Very peaceful." Said Malik.

"Yes, well, you have an ID., please?"

"Right here," said Malik and handed them his Ga. license which he'd fished out of his wallet. His hands were bigger than Dimarks, wider, plumper, wrinkled skin, old hands!

Dimarks took the license and turned it over, back over and stared at it for a long time. "Do you own this land?" He waved his hand toward the marsh and spit of land.

"Not at all, but friends own it," Malik smiled. And that is the truth. "I mean, it belongs to a close friend."

"So, this land is owned by Alona Lois...." Dimarks trailed off..."and you stay here with her permission?" Dimarks already knew who the land belonged to, of course. He already knew the taxes were paid and on time. The lady who owned it was a widow. He knew all about her.

"Correct," said Malik.

"What are you driving?"

"I'm driving a red Ford F 150," said Malik.

"Where is it?" asked Dimarks.

"It's in the shop right now, getting a new set of tires put on," said Malik. "I've got a ride coming to take me to get the truck," Malik looked at his watch, "And I need to get my things together to get the truck and go back up the coast."

"He asked how long you'd been in the state," asked the shorter agent, whose name tag said, Force Hilland, III, and Malik smiled. What a crazy sounding name!

"I'm a foreigner but I've been in the good ole USA all my life. Born in Savannah to legally documented, immigrant parents. One sister, two brothers. My parents are Jewish and came here from Israel."

Malik took a deep breath. "They owned land and were farmers."

He got up carefully from the rocking chair and stood back, holding onto the rocking chair. He was old and creaky like senior citizens get, like it or not, here was old age!

"Now if you gentlemen don't mind, my ride will be here any minute and I need to get my things and lock the door here," said Malik.

The men nodded and Dimarks said, "Okay. We'll see you around. Take it easy."

Agent Force said, "See ya," and the agents ambled out to their black SUV and got in and sat there. And sat there, talking. Watching.

Which was okay by Malik because he did indeed have a ride coming, that would take him down the road to pick up his truck so he could head back to Savannah, Ga. up the coast.

He had a place to stay there, a nice condo, big screen television, great restaurants nearby. Tybee Island is just a stone's throw to the east of his condo, and he fully intended to take a break and just vegetate in the sun for a few days.

And Tybee Island, beautiful like here but not this beautiful, was where he was headed after a short rest at the condo.

Tybee. Oh, how he loved the sound of the word that described another favorite place on the coast Tybee Island, Georgia.

He wanted to launch the project there at Tybee Island, over the causeway from Savannah, Georgia. His plans were written down in a small notebook.

This was a mission, not just a project off the wall, but God led. It was his calling to be born and live in a time such as now. And this mission was his heart. He was excited. He loved what he was about to do.

The agent's car pulled out of the drive and left Big Daddy Island. They drove slowly of course, because the road leading into this paradise was thick dirt and sandy as a dust bowl.

Malik was glad of that. Glad they were leaving. On these missions Malik went on, it was always something. And although the supernatural side of Malik was patient and long suffering as a mama feeding five kids on goat milk and crackers, the earthly part of Malik, the human side, if you will, was weary.

His times on this crazier than ever earth had worn him out as though he was at the tail end of a marathon, sweating like a boar hog. Malik had never been, that he could recall, this tired. Man, he was exhausted! And because he was so plain tired, he went inside the Cabin called Yellow on Big Daddy Island and took a nap.

He sprawled on the army cot, and he did not move a hair, and the silver hair was soon plastered onto the white pillow. The nap was restful but a bad idea. He dreamed but was half awake which meant it was more of a nightmare than anything else. It had noise and distraction, oh my!

And yes, the nightmare came to life and then some. He had answered God, with "Send me!"

and he was here at the happy place for sure, but there was more to come. No dull moments.

It was July, sweltering coastal Georgia heat and the monstrous skeeters were already buzzing every leg and arm! Humidity was torture! But, ah, summer in the Georgia coast, no better laid-back attitude anywhere on earth! But it was not attitude enough to stop the women.

Nor the principle, If it can go wrong, it might.

Chapter 3:
Where the Girls Are

Because that is when the ladies showed up. The pair who was always up to something, good mostly but curious and after him, no doubt.

The nightmare was real. And it was growing by the minute! Man, everybody was here!

Malik had been dreaming he was being pursued by two ladies who were fit to kill. And might. Because the truth was, Malik was a squatter due to, no, he did not have permission to stay here.

He stayed here because he loved it. He moved into Yellow when he came down to the coast, or simply needed thinking space. Yellow, and this land, once upon a time was in his family. Oh my, seemed like yesterday. When he was not here, he longed to be here.

But things were different now. Now, he had to be sneaky about it, so the island owner, Alona Lois, didn't find out. She had a best friend, of course, a petite blonde. Mercedes, who was hell on those Cadillac wheels she drove, and the last thing Malik needed (the first thing this fine morning) there's that line of lyrics again, Malik smiled and wondered if he was going to have to give Willie Nelson all his money, then laughed.

The truth is no. LOL. Malik had met and smoked one with Willie one time in a little one stop light town somewhere in North Texas and considered him his friend. But that's another story, Malik thought, rolling over.

He crawled off the army cot and pulled on his Wellingtons. He grabbed his baseball cap. He heard the ladies talking. They were sneaking up to the cabin. They were behind Yellow and started tapping on the thin walls. Dear Jesus, Malik hissed.

The window was open. "He's in there, I can smell armpits on a man a mile away," Mercedes said and tapped the wall. She laughed and Alona Lois joined in.

They giggled louder. Now, this is funny, they thought. Then tried to hush. Why is it, the older you get the funnier stupid stuff gets? And they considered this plain stupid. Imagine an interloper in Yellow. How brave--or doped up--the man was! Mental? They were about to find out! Mercedes rattled the yellow painted walls like firing off buckshot. Furiously. "Yee haw, company's coming!" she yelled. Tap, tap, tap rapidly. Tap, tap!

She and Alona Lois had talked about this day and night for a few days since the Sheriff's office contacted Alona Lois about the intruder. The Chief Deputy assured her they would find out who the interloper was and get back with her. But you know how slowly the wheels of investigations go. I mean, come on!

On the waterways of the marsh beyond the edge of Big Daddy Island, a kayaker had gotten lost and was flapping water trying to turn around. Good luck with that! thought Alona Lois.

Of course, Mercedes insisted they go down to Big Daddy Island and smoke the guy out, if needed or make enough racket to scare him into coming out. Talk with him, have him put in jail?

Something! At least find out who he was and what his purpose was there, interloping.

Mercedes said, 'Whoever he is, might need our help!" She kind of hoped so, she had a need to help!

"I'm not sure who this is, we've never seen him before," said Alona Lois. "And he's going to get my help alright, the taxes on this place are outrageous. If he wants to rent, we'll talk about it, but homeless people don't have rent money! Furthermore, it's a different day and time from what we grew up in; man might be dangerous. Could be a felon!"

"But God might be sending us to help someone," Mercedes argued, knowing Alona Lois was into helping others but she didn't abide or thieves or cheaters! She wasn't about to help someone into terrorizing them, or vandalizing or using illegally, this island get-away, or the work done before. It all belonged to her and the daughters, and four grandchildren!

Right now, here they were, ready to roll the stranger's head! Both were grandma's and neither cared what the trespasser was doing. He had to go! For insurance purposes, and other concerns, the man could not camp here. County laws wouldn't tolerate it.

Alona Lois and Mercedes were dressed for the manhunt: camo jeans, t-shirts, shawls, and yard boots they called it. Mercedes had a stick in one hand and Alona Lois had a pistol in a holster at her hip and carried a walking stick in her right hand.

They were Senior Citizens although neither one looked a day over 50-60 and neither one of them would back down from a fight over their island here. They loved this place, and it was their responsibility to protect it.

Especially Alona lois. She had inherited it from her husband who passed away some years prior. She had promised to protect and care for the island. Mercedes of course, their closest friend, felt like it was partly hers, she smiled, although her name was not on the deed her heart was. She had come to love Alona Lois like a sister, no, a lot closer. They thought alike and she often said they were "twins!" They had each other's backs.

She rattled the window now, a small rectangle of glass. She tapped it with the big ring on her right hand and Alona Lois pulled her hand back.

She said nothing, just shook her head.

Inside the cabin, Malik's eyes were wide. The women were here as he knew they would be. He coughed, "his girls" (which is what he called his daughters) and them too. You know, they are your "girls". Smile. He smiled and could have pounded his own skull for the interruptions!

How would he explain being here? He did not know, just that he better think and be quick about it. Women are harder to deal with than those feds, he thought. And these women were smart. He wasn't going to outwit them.

Malik also knew the women were deep thinkers and dedicated Christians, both good folks. It would take a front-end loader to lift a curse word from their lips and although they leaned toward saving all the animals they found and doing for others at every turn, the fact was that wool could not be pulled over their eyes.

He said a prayer that now, at this late time in all of existence, what could he say to comfort them? Thinking he needed to get out of here and on with the mission, Malik tucked in his blue Polo shirt, buckled his brass belt buckle with the tractor embossed on it and stepped outside onto the small porch. Might as well jump into a frying pan, he thought, trying to smile.

"What in the world?" he shouted as Alona Lois and Mercedes peeked around the corner of Yellow.

Alona Lois and Mercedes went, "Ohhhh! And their mouths dropped open, and they held onto the wall to keep from fainting!

Chapter 4:

The Stranger

Startling moments. Moments in life when the spirit which rocks the world, stills our heartbeats almost to nil, and we can't move this way or that. Literally, can't move. Everything we thought we knew is handed to us in broken pieces by unseen hands. And the "everything we thought we knew" we don't know and in its place is truth. Suddenly we understand a mystery of life we never understood before. When we stand before the oak wood casket (or pine) of a precious mother or father, a child gone too soon, a son or daughter who was our mini-me, we could not save, the agony is unbearable. But, watching them descend into the earth, we understand the power of life.

Things are bigger than us, simplified. Life and death. There is, indeed, a beyond.

This was such a moment for Malikhan Sharon and Alona Lois and Mercedes. Standing on the porch of Yellow, on the edge of a marsh teeming with unseen life the moment teemed with memories and a question mark.

They were stunned and at the same time their spirits rejoiced, and they knew this stranger and were known by him. Suddenly they got it.

"The human part of the ladies wanted to ask Who is this man? The spirit whispered YOU KNOW.

Malik smiled. Of course, they knew, as he knew. He was on a mountain that reached the blue Georgia skies. He had always known. And what you know can hurt you!

Alona Lois was wide eyed, her brown eyes serious yet smiling, her mouth open slightly, stunned, right. Her platinum blonde hair (no gray for her) was cut below her chin. She wore a smile though deep down she was cautious.

Mercedes, who kept her long hair platinum blonde too, stared through stormy blue eyes and felt the higher power surround them.

Malik wanted to laugh but he knew it would sound hoarse. He was 6' 1" tall but felt short. He was human and both knees hurt as did his back. He coughed and covered his mouth with a big hand with swollen joints. Old, okay?

I didn't know what this would be like, thought Alona Lois and glanced at Mercedes. This can't be who and what I think. But she knew it was. Every ounce of her felt crazy bold and she relaxed. Just accept it, she sighed. It is what it is.

She had heard of people dancing in the spirit (never at the Methodist Church she attended) and she had a yen to go outside and dance on the dock to the music of the marsh. Birds. Rising tides. Boats in the distance.

Mercedes glanced sideways and she wasn't speaking words. Rare. Mercedes felt like dancing in the spirit, dancing on the dock to the music of the marsh. Two besties thinking alike.

They were old at this moment, in their height of life, and they followed each other outside and crossed to the wooden dock which cut a long narrow path outward, into the hands of the marsh. They needed to have a word or two. Alone.

The two ladies wept as they stepped onto the beloved wooden dock. They walked, which appeared as dancing down the dock. They tapped their feet and swayed their arms. Dressed in camo jeans and black t shirts (Mercedes wearing a camo shawl) Alona Lois wearing a t-shirt over the black shirt, with a golf cart on it and this: *In Augusta, this is how we roll,* and they moved to the end of the dock. They giggled and smelled fish and mud.

They sighed and laughed and pretended to sing. They gazed at the emerald and peridot green marsh laid out like shag carpet.

Malikhan Sharon came onto the dock, hobbling and using his walking cane with a silver Corvette knob on it. He too, felt the music of the marsh, the sea and the forever which surrounded them. This place was paradise, a dream to love.

The ladies were exhausted from their unreal dancing in the spirit moment. Alona Lois would laugh about the whole thing and Mercedes would tell anyone who listened, how they had been "caught up in the spirit" which sounds so Southern doesn't it? And everyone would laugh, and it would feel so, so good.

Malik spoke. "I think you ladies think you know me, but you don't." He was on a mission, remember, his dream mission, and he must see it through!

"Well, you look like someone we both knew, not long ago, either!" said Alona Lois.

Malik's silver hair glistened in the early July morning, and his brown eyes shone with love.

They loved it here and he loved it here. Friends know these things.

"I am on a mission and just dropped by to rest a few nights here. I love this place," he said and meant it. He swept a tan arm toward the island behind them. Toward the marsh before them.

"We love it too and she owns the place," said Mercedes, pointing to Alona Lois. "You remind us of her husband who died, and my best friend of course," Mercedes patted Alona Lois's hand.

"He was my best friend but she and the one you remind us of, were married a long time!"

"You are a lot like him, the man from our past, very similar, same height, color of eyes," Alona Lois said. "You act like he acted. It seems unreal!"

"But that doesn't mean you are him!" said Mercedes, "so we were checking this out."

"Do you want to rent the place?" Asked Alona Lois, and added, "because it's not for rent. I only let my daughters and grandkids visit Big Daddy Island and take the boat out. The white boat.

My son in law drives the boat. And they wear life jackets! And Mercedes naturally. She helps me see after the place."

"Oh no! I'm leaving. I was going to drive the truck parked, but I know it's in the shop. Not sure how I'll get up to Savannah now to launch my mission. Malik sighed and shrugged his wide shoulders.

"Are you a missionary?" asked Mercedes.

"No, no missionary, well sort of," said Malik.

"It's my life's calling to do this. I'm going on a mission to save pets! I love animals!"

"My mother saved S and H Green stamps," said Mercedes. All three laughed. "She also bought magazines from Publisher's Clearing House, and almost to the day she left this world she was watching for that white van and the flowers and man with the big check!"

"Fur-babies!" said Alona Lois. "How great. I've got dogs and donkeys in my field and all sorts of animals around," hmmm, she murmured thinking. I love pets too. I want to rescue them.

Her brown eyes smiled at the thought of Malik's mission. Strange name, she thought, but could not ignore the fact of saving animals! What a great idea! Alona Lois loved animals!

"Hmmmm," uttered Mercedes. "That's something I've always wanted to do." And she meant it. She had begged others to help her establish a pet sanctuary, or a rescue. No takers.

"How do you know which ones to save?" asked Alona Lois. "I love this idea, but we'd like to talk about it later. Back to you staying here, you can't stay here!" She shifted from one foot to the other.

"We really know you, but we don't know you. I think you jolted us and took us back to our memories and we get a little wild sometimes."

"I won't come back," said Malik and thought, right. This is my last time here, how sad!

"He won't come back," said Mercedes. hoping, knowing he would. How easy to know this about the man who looked like Alona Lois's husband for real, maybe a lot older, and Mercedes's true and

kind best friend in all the world for longer than she would care to admit.

"Why don't you ladies go with me to Savannah and help me with the mission?" said Malik and his eyes widened at the suggestion because you readers see, this was NOT part of Malik's great plans. It was a monkey wrench, but not part of the plans, at all. He blurted this out and he never blurted things out. He surprised himself that he was so much of the world of humans!

"Why don't you ride with us back up there?" asked Mercedes. Mercedes and Alona Lois had driven down to Big Daddy Island in Alona Lois's red pick-up truck. The truck was like the one she kept there at Big Daddy Island, a Ford F-150. (Which was in fact, in a local shop for repairs.)

"I have a condo, but you can't stay there."

"Wherever you stay we could have dinner and talk about this mission you are about to go on, which sounds like my heart talking," said Mercedes. "We could get together." How about a date, is what she wanted to ask. Ha, ha, ha.

"How do you figure to support your travels?" asked Alona Lois. She was all business, smart.

"I'm going to take up donations, maybe a Go fund me," said Malik. Although he didn't say it, he already had funds. He had stones and felt the cool jade hanging from a silver chain around his neck. (Remember?) and the stones were powerful, in areas of healing, finding, saving stones.

"Well, okay," said Alona Lois. Normally an every "I" dotted type person but she was old, okay.

Her days were numbered like the days of these other wild cats, and she felt adventure ahead.

She smiled. She felt compelled to know more about Malik, because he did remind her of her late husband she loved beyond life. Life seems to get crazier by the day, doesn't it, she thought, as she and Mercedes walked back down to the end of the dock, across the yard to the red Ford truck and got in. They waited.

Malik could sit behind the shotgun side, in the second seat. They waited and laughed and laughed and slapped their knees. Feeling good.

The laughter felt good, and it got too loud. Alona Lois blew her nose on a Kleenex. Mercedes cried and gagged. They had been up much of the night but neither felt tired. On the trip to Savannah, they would grill Malik. They had often called themselves, "grill masters" and he was nice enough.

A little crazy but hey, Mercedes reminded Alona Lois how they had been at a golf club reception a few years back, in a room of crazy people, thinking they were the only ones sane. And Alona Lois laughed that time and said, "Yes, but we've been wrong before." Which they still laughed about to this day.

My goodness, the whole world was mad. They were Senior Citizens and the idea of them chasing down an interloper and now getting tangled up with his mission to save animals was a twist of events, but a great idea! They loved it like bad coffee made from old tires. At least, the smell, tee-hee.   Neither of the ladies liked yoga. Neither liked exercise except for walking, which they both loved.   Saving animals is healthy! As we age, we seem to run out of worthy things to do, literally. We must find causes to foster and participate in. Here could be something! Alona Lois said to

Mercedes, "If this guy tries anything funny give me a signal, say something like, My Lord have mercy, I've got to scratch my rash," something like that and I'll know he's about to do something!" I can handle it.

Mercedes laughed, "He's alright. I can feel it."

"You are the judge then, just stay alert and we'll drive him back to Savannah and put him out wherever he wants to go, meet later maybe, maybe not." Alona Lois planned to let it shake out.

"Yes, but we want to see him and get involved in his mission. I've always wanted to save fur babies…people are so mean!" exclaimed Mercedes. "And I already have a lot I've rescued," she rolled her eyes.

"Well if he's serious, we'll know shortly! I just wonder how and what he's going to do to fund this!" Alona Lois rolled her eyes.

"I know, just be patient. We'll find out."

Malik approached the truck with a duffle bag in his left hand. Alona Lois wondered what was in it. She hopped out and opened the back door, took the bag, and dropped it onto the seat behind them. She did this because she knew about weapons. She wanted to feel the bag to see how heavy it was.

Not heavy at all. She smiled. Good.

Malik crawled up and into the Ford truck. They drove out of the gate to Big Daddy Island and headed up SR 99 to Savannah. And on the way to the southern city of art and romance, which was not burned by Sherman because he had told the Union soldiers, the city was too beautiful to burn, the ladies found out a lot more about Malik than they wanted.

And it got crazier by the minute.

Chapter 5:

The Trip

Beneath the Georgia skies, the July morning golden, red, pink sun unfurled like a pleated fan. The fan twitched, held in the gloved fingers of an Antebellum lady dressed in a thousand yards of blue skirt. Along the bottom, at the hem almost touching the ground, rode a pod of sharks. The gray fins spiked thunder clouds into the blue skirt.

Which meant or did not mean (anyone living on the coast knows) it might rain, or storm, or it might not.

Peggy Mercer

Alona Lois was lost in thought as she he stared at the road. The truck drove smoothly, and her pedal stayed on the metal.

Malik's stories made for great filler material for the trip. This felt like a chapter or verse of a country music song, Mercedes thought.

Alona Lois was convinced she and Mercedes were going to dig up background on Malik by the time they got him to Savannah and out to Tybee Island. There were many questions for this man who resembled her dead husband! I'll get to the bottom of this guy who has me shook up! I'll find out how he knew in the first place, about Big Daddy Island.

Who gave him permission to stay overnight in Yellow? Keep your priorities straight girl, herself said, and don't let this silver-tongued talker, (Silver haired, she smiled a crooked smile) talk you into something you may regret!

Alona Lois maneuvered the truck in and out of traffic on SR 99, headed up the coast. She enjoyed the sing-song chatter of Mercedes, trying to get info out of Malik. Almost funny what stuff you can get talked into. At her age, a lot of her thoughts were gloomy, and she was aware of her short time left on this planet! She and Mercedes talked about this all the time. Her brown eyes widened at a rabbit darting across the road, and she shook her head, platinum hair bobbing at her jaw.

She pressed her lips together, seriously no, and no, again! It was not funny at all--this aging stuff. To her, it was the biggest surprise of life!

Alona Lois, while a well-known lady and well liked, in the area, was a lonely woman. Her few great friendships meant the world to her, and she relied on those friendships to lead her through some scary moments. She loved Mercedes like a sister. She and Mercedes were life to one another!

Mercedes laughed at something silly. She declared she was so hungry "she could eat a cow," but Alona Lois knew this friend well. Her eyes were always bigger than her tummy.

Malik said, "Y'all ladies want to stop for lunch?" And the way he spoke, y'all with a fake drawl, was hilarious. It was like "y" then AWE "l" rolling, stuttering, killing the "l" --well, silly man.

He'd said he was from Savannah, which meant Southern, but Alona Lois knew better. He was no more southern than a snowbird. She didn't believe a word of it. Mercedes fell for anything and everything, but one of them (and that meant her) Alona Lois, had to think with common sense! She had never been into the drama of Mercedes, which was one thing she loved about her. She was like a child in many ways and Alona Lois loved children!

But this man here, who was he? Whomever, she was taken back to a time long ago. A time when Big Daddy was her life. The man she missed most in the midnight hours. Malik was his twin!

Their life together was a time of love, with two daughters and a son, some late life heartbreak which seems to be a part of most marriages, and for them, disappointments, right. She was the good girl, the southern lady, the good mama and now trying to be the good grandmama.

She had been a good wife, and he had been a husband with a yen to wander. She knew why. Though others never understood her tolerance, she understood him. And she let him go free and he of course, kept coming back to her and their home and their condo in Savannah, also Big Daddy Island. So, it went. They loved each other.

Tears slipped from Alona Lois's eyes. Though she didn't weep easily, she felt tears, cool as water fresh drawn from a well slide down her left cheek. Good thing she was driving so the others could not see it, she thought. Tears, huh?

She frowned. Wonder where this is coming from? Well, Malik's nearness, brought back memories of the man I loved, Big Daddy.

These memories, while painful, gave her peace and calm. Her power to rise above the memories was because Alona Lois had always done the right thing. She kept her family tied together and when he died, she was the one by his side, as God meant it to be.

She was happy too, because of this stranger's talk of new adventure. His mission. He was talking about his God ordained mission of saving fur babies, which was something she had always wanted to do. All put together, it was an odd twist of fate, but when you are old enough to know better is when it's more fun, right?

Due to working her fulltime job as a rural mail carrier (making good money for sure), but long hours, Alona Lois had no time for extracurricular activities. Looking back, she wished she had developed a serious hobby or mission of some sort.

But Alona Lois had never felt called to a hobby or cause because the job she had was hot, sweaty, exhausting and demanding. No time for anything else except maybe helping with the grandkids as they came along.

She now wished for a greater purpose in life. Close friends had suggested she get involved with "something" but what?

Right now, her idea was to find lunch. Then, drive to Savannah, deliver Malik and maybe supper. By then she might help launch his mission to save animals! This excited her.

She might find motivation after all! At least she was retired and could get into projects! She laughed and wondered where he planned to put the saved animals.

Not her house. She had a pair of donkeys, cats, dogs, chickens --you name it! But for the first time in a long time, Alona Lois felt excited about Malik's mission. Not only did she wish him the best, she may help this handsome silver-haired old hunk who stirred longings of her late husband. He was a Southern Gentleman, like Big Daddy had been. Oh, my word!

Looking back, she had wished for a boyfriend, but it seemed too late in life. She smiled, now there was a thought. Now it might not be.

Alona Lois was older and although Mercedes kept telling her to keep the hair platinum and never let a gray hair show, she looked a lot younger. She was adamant about planning activities and everything working out as it should. In the red Ford F-150, Mercedes riding shotgun and Malik a twin for her late husband, talking like he belonged with them. Alona Lois tried to plan. But, if she had only known what was ahead, she would not have planned a thing. She would have put the truck into reverse!

Mercedes loved the sound of the big truck tires rolling along SR 99. She loved memories of times she had fairly flown up and down this highway, loving the coast and stopping at the Marina north of Darien, or seafood restaurants. She loved her blue and white boat, the *Sea Y'all lady*, kept at the private Marina. She loved taking the boat for rides across the North River, out to Doboy Sound to the dock at Sapelo Island. Sometimes the rides turned topsy turvy with angry waves. The sea talked the language of sailors and water walkers. She loved this Georgia coast. She felt it was like the shores of Gennesarat in Israel, where our Lord and Savior walked on water. What was he thinking, on those long walks, Mercedes wondered.

Of the forthcoming times which would rock the earth like being shattered by hurled stones? The man was talking. He had claimed his name was Malikhan Sharon, but she didn't believe it. Not for a minute. She knew she was jumping before she was poked but she didn't care. She, Mercedes, who believed from her first breath on earth –

prayed over by faith-filled Bible belt worshipping loved ones—believed this guy was a ghost from the beyond. She believed in the higher power. God's power was the greatest!

One of these days, mountains would crumble to the sea and the Georgia blue skies would open! A voice was going to beckon them from on high!

A trumpet, angels, the whole works, exactly as it had been prophesied! Oh Glory!

As we know it, she, Mercedes, believed in the Supernatural power of the Father in Heaven. Her heartbeat was faster as she listened to this man's voice. It was such a familiar voice—a bit hoarse and his laugh was a giggle-- she could not think of words to encrypt it. No words to describe the familiarity. Too uncanny. It had to be Supernatural, had to be!

To Mercedes, this guy was too much like Alona's husband, and her best friend, what? She paused her brain. Where am I going with this wild thinking? This can't be true. This can't be real!

The husband of Alona Lois was six feet under the red Georgia dirt, at a cemetery in the hills of North Ga., and he sure wasn't coming back! No way. She had been to the grave and would go again. Big Daddy was there, not here with them! But this guy Malik, a sweet man who looked, acted, and talked in a similar voice much like the husband and friend had talked; looked like an older version of him too. Tall, six feet one and broad shouldered, big hands, hair as silver as tears falling from the blue sky, but this could not, no way, hey now, NO! NOT HI!

Then again this was your gal, Mercedes, who loved mystery and drama and strange twists to stories. WHO was he then? A twin? A visitor from another planet? Who? Her mind ran the gamut from alien to visitor from Mars.

They covered the miles up SR 99, hugging the Georgia coast. The Ford truck rolled as easily as the blue and white boat, the *Sea Y'all Lady,* sailed the steely waters of Doboy Sound.

The Ford F150 was Alona Lois's truck but had been HIS truck and she and Alona Lois often went thrifting in the truck. This truck pulled the boats to the water. It pulled Alona Lois's tractor and lawn mower to Big Daddy Island. It hauled!

They were traveling in class (for country folks, that is), and the sound of Malik's voice rose above the din of wheels and gave her cold chills.

Oh yes, Mercedes had said she was hungry enough to eat a cow, and which Alona Lois glanced at her sideways, smiling, knowing Mercedes always said she was starving but was never that hungry. Malik had asked if they wanted to stop and "Get some lunch," and laughed.

"There are great restaurants along this road, just pick one!' said Alona Lois from the driver's seat. "And all over Savannah!"

"I'm not waiting till we get to Savannah to eat!" said Mercedes.

"Wherever you girls want to stop. Lunch is on me," said Malik. Both girls wondered how it was that he could afford, in these inflated times, springing for three lunches. Alona Lois and Mercedes both thought Malik was retired from something good. His hair was silver. He was old enough they knew, and he was creaky and old, so yes, retired. And going to spend the money.

Alona Lois could also afford to buy everyone's lunch. She had retired from a full-time, lucrative job which secured her, plus she was indeed, the widow of this man's "twin" and benefitted from having had a husband. The late husband and her had married young and done well. Worked their butts off for sure but amounted to something with money in the bank. And she did own Big Daddy Island plus if you must know, other "islands."

Mercedes didn't dare volunteer to pay for the food. She was afraid of her one credit card and didn't dare splurge. But she was such a happy spirit people's opinion of her was rich.

If only they knew. Now she did own her own home in Georgia in a little bitty town inland. She did have that. She had property although it needed repairs. What else does a person need, she often thought, a roof, warm socks and shoes, food, health! Goodness! Music, books, pets! Ah yes.

"I just do not want McDonald's junk," said Mercedes and Alona Lois laughed. "You can say that again!"

"I don't like their food either," said Malik.

"We need good food, I'm on a diet to try and get my cholesterol down!" said Mercedes.

"I'm not on a diet but I need to be," said Alona Lois. "I take bp medicine but need to eat better! I need to eat healthier foods!"

"Me too," said Malik and giggled.

Mercedes loved the easy-going small talk. It was like they had known this guy forever; words were friendly, and easy between the three. What makes this feeling of knowing someone forever?

The Traveler

At a younger age, neither Alona Lois nor Mercedes would have given a stranger a ride to Savannah. But way back then, is not here and now, and they had more courage and felt more adventurous in their old days. As we age, we are more up for taking chances. We feel we have less to lose; why not?

The road they drove, SR 99, hugged the beautiful Georgia coast and on the right side between them and the ocean sprawled salt-water marshland, thick with stands of cypress trees live oaks and pines.

Fishing villages seemed out of another era and spread out among Loblolly pines on either side of SR 99. Trailer homes and campers belonging to fishermen who came from all over, sat quietly, unoccupied (Gone fishing) and a quiet and peaceful atmosphere marked the mood.

This scenic tour road winds its way along one of the last rustic coastlines in the USA. One might see a bald eagle soaring above the cypress trees. One might hear the tapping of a pileated woodpecker or see a regal heron flying above the marsh. Colors of green browns, golds swayed in the summer breeze. Fiddler crabs scurried about, feasting in the sprawling mudflats, finding food, contributing to the life of the swamps and marshland.

Mercedes was excited. The three riders in the truck were oddly silent, each enjoying the scenery. The Georgia coastal region is other worldly, with swamps and marshlands teeming with birds and animals, owning the ocean shorelines.

One third of the entire Atlantic salt-water marshland is within the Georgia coast. The white clapboard houses beside SR 99, where Guale might have lived, and descendants still do -- some have porches painted in traditional "haint blue" to scare off evil spirits-- are historic. Dear Lord, Mercedes

The Traveler

loved every mile of it. She loved stopping to take photographs! There was a quaint sea food restaurant up the road, and Mercedes asked to stop there for lunch. "Let's stop at Hungry House!" she squealed, "it's just a few more miles!"

Hungry House had been named for the song Elvira, by the Oak Ridge Boys and since Mercedes was their biggest fan, she could close her eyes and hear Richard Sterban singing Ooom paw paw! The food at Hungry House was to die for.

Alona Lois said, "Ok." She had eaten there before and agreed. The food was wonderful.

She loved the shrimp battered in a buttermilk mix and there was no seafood you could not get. They gave you big bibs and you needed them! Plenty of paper towels to wipe your hands (and mouth). And several pitchers of sweet tea.

Malik giggled. "I've eaten there. Great seafood, yes, one of my favorites. Yes, stop there."

Alona Lois's exact thoughts. Seemed he was reading her mind or had been there (with her) before. Nonsense thinking, she thought, but smiled anyhow. Mercedes acted starving. But this little Hungry House, as they called it, Restaurant, would fix that. Nobody left hungry!

To the right, they passed a sprawling marshland, reminding her of Big Daddy Island which also bordered. sprawling marshland and was within yelling distance of the Sapelo workstation.

This "island" land they owned (well, Alona Lois), was paradise and to Mercedes, her happy place. Their place of memories!

The Traveler

For Alona Lois the island held wonderful, but sometimes painful memories. It was paradise with a capital **P**. Her family loved it.

Mercedes loved the place which also held wonderful but sometimes painful memories. Mercedes prayed Hollywood and the millionaire stars would stay away. She prayed nobody found out about the blessed Georgia coastline. A place out of time, like stepping into a slower life, a slower moving of the hands on the clocks of existence. Peace, harmony, no noise…oh Joy, what a place it was!

She was excited about this stranger, Malik Sharon, who was interloping on Big Daddy Island, sleeping in Yellow like he owned it! He seemed to love it as they did, the majestic palm trees and the pretzel shaped limbs of the live oaks with beards.

In times past, she would never have given him a ride anywhere, had him thrown in jail was more like it, but like Alona Lois, he reminded her of Big Daddy, oh yes, he did!

She missed Big Daddy most in the summertime. She knew Alona Lois missed him most late at night when she became lonelier than usual. Wives who are widows say nights are the hardest!

Mercedes, like Alona Lois, had made her mind up to See Malik got to wherever he was going in Savannah, then maybe meet him on Tybee to launch his saving fur baby's mission.

Mercedes thought the project heartwarming and exciting. She knew it would work. Feeding and caring for animals is physically and mentally exhausting at times, but she was all in. It was an idea she would have done sooner if she'd had any muscle power handy. But she didn't.

God calls us to these works. And while they might get you into the Pearly Gates, and on toward your degree of Glory where you will live out your eternal existence, every dream of every person on earth requires tons of hard work.

She and Alona Lois were not gold medal contenders--Senior citizens, hard to believe, I know, right--and she only had so much strength and power. She knew this but the project Malik was about to launch was exciting! She loved helping and since she'd been born and raised on a farm near the Satilla River, Mercedes loved creatures. Dogs, cats, mules, donkeys, goats, chickens—little yellow biddies with tiny feathers—oh goodness she was an animal lover bar none!

However, as she and Alona Lois had learned fast, rescuing animals, whether dog, cat, or other animals, is not always easy. Always more to it than meets the eye, Mercedes thought. In her car, she had a leash, carrier and cans of food and bottled water. Just in case she found a hungry or lost dog or cat. Mercedes was the queen of rescuing animals.

Sometimes she found herself overwhelmed with the rescues, but she figured out new homes and good ones or she kept them. Which meant her house had a fence around it and nobody dared walk through her yard.

"The restaurant is about four miles is all," said Alona Lois looking sideways at Mercedes briefly. Her platinum hair bobbed.

Mercedes said, "Well I can eat a cow." She was hungry and Malik had said a few miles back, that he was paying so she could get what she wanted. No studying the menu for prices! Nothing was off the table!

"Yay!" She loved seafood and Hungry House was the place south of the Tea Line that sold the best seafood in Georgia.

The three of them would stop and eat their fill, chat about Malik's mission of saving animals. Mercedes and Alona Lois planned to dig into specifics, looking to solve some questions. They needed details if they wound up helping Malik! I should say, and how!

Seemed such an easy plan. In her life, Mercedes had rescued many animals! Nothing to it, just grab them, feed them, and find them loving homes. Or as she was prone, keep them!

Right now, all she wanted was stop and eat and get to the details. They were all dressed nicely.

The ladies in their camo jeans and black shirts looked professional and the new man of the hour, Malikhan Sharon looked nice to be a Senior, ha ha. He was her type for sure. He was also Alona Lois's type. Or any woman's type! Southern Gentleman.

Stop and eat, stop and eat, her stomach growled. She could smell the food and they were not even there yet!

They rode along, falling quiet, thinking about the lunch they were about to have, the restaurant ahead a few miles. Simple.

How could anything go wrong? wondered Mercedes? Don't mess with Texas, or me!

Indeed. She saw Malik was lost in thought!

The Traveler

And he was. In the amazing grace of his last mile home, in the yearning to see lights in the window where he'd been raised, and beneath the burden of the mission before him which God had ordained, Malik cried big silent tears, squinting and hoping they would stop before the ladies saw him and started asking questions.

He wept stones, so hard were the tears. He wept crashing waves on jagged rocks!

In the maze of many missions, over the course of callings from God in Heaven, as the times of his earthly being became clear in this moment, like a twinkling of God's unseen eye, Malik felt his oats.

He was quiet in this thinking.

Mercedes jumped into his deep thinking, "The restaurant is only another mile. I'm unhooking my seat belt!"

"No don't do that," said Alona Lois.

"I'm kind of hungry," said Malik. He wiped his face with his tan hands.

He was excited for sure. He was hungry, born of flesh and blood, the body had to eat didn't it? He was thirsty too. He believed in the power of fasting and fasted often, but not now, Lord, please! He smiled and even God the Father knew how his body needed a little sugar and some good salt.

He had a slight headache and a wearisome dry cough which never left him. It was better, however, on this trip to the Golden Isles and up the coast! The Golden Isles of Georgia are not dubbed "golden" for nothing. Both the islands' sunrises and sunsets seem liquid fire, pouring gold on the sugary white sands of the Georgia barrier islands.

There are no golden sunsets like it anywhere else! No starry nights to compare!

As they pulled into the sandy, seashell edged yard of the Hungry House Restaurant on the right side of highway 17, near Shellman Bluff, Georgia, Malik felt longing in the hollow of his memories.

The measure of a man's life on earth is the good he does; the marks he makes. The actions.

Oh, he had lived normal lives as everybody calls it on earth. Malik had enjoyed friends. Like now, The two ladies were something else. His thoughts were interrupted as he got out of the truck and fished out a cane. He followed Alona Lois and Mercedes into the shack of a building with the acre-wide front porch.

This is where Cracker Barrell must have gotten their idea for porch chairs because Malik counted ten wooden rocking chairs, pinch apart. Every porch in these parts had a pair of rocking chairs. Some have more than one pair!

Mercedes said, "Come on, we can rock on the way out!"

Alona Lois and Mercedes eased through the front, wide glass door and into the restaurant, which was feeding four customers. Four men dressed in black suits, sitting at a wooden table, facing the river beyond, chatting up a storm.

It was 11:00 o'clock in the morning and they had been up since sunrise and the four men must be the before the lunch group. They sat at a table with their backs to the crowd so they could see beyond the big picture window to the river and parking area to the left side.

Malik could not see their faces, but in his gut, a red flag waved!

Shellman Bluff sits on the Broro and Julienton Rivers. It is an old fish camp village and home to about 7800 residents. It is laid back area, a place for those who love to fish and chill, seine for shrimp and play music!

One movie star owned a beautiful house near the high bluff, but most homes were trailer houses, small cottages, some not more than sheds with a parking spot.

I hope they keep it this way, Malik thought as a waitress walked up.

The waitress carried a cloth over one arm, regal like, and a menu in her head, broad brow, bushy eyebrows, perfect teeth, the two in front solid gold. A band around her head.

The smell of grits and waffles from the kitchen!

In a southern drawl that would forever keep her from making it in the movies, the waitress announced every meal available.

Her gold teeth flashed like caution lights. Malik wondered if she was a descendant of the Guale, which most in this area were. Her rich voice with the sing song lyrical tones said, yes, I'm Geechee.

Tinkling music came from the front, near the windows where a man wearing a white shirt and white cotton pants played a battered piano. Another man stood beside him, wearing a jacket, a jazz cap on his head and playing a guitar softly and a younger man with an Afro tapped a set of tall Conga drums. The Hungry House Trio.

At Hungry House Restaurant, visitors have their rocking chairs on the porch, smell the food within a half mile of the place and it smells like a kitchen in Heaven, and your friends pack in for the seafood, fresh and fried to perfection.

If you can name it and it comes from the Atlantic Ocean, then Hungry House serves it.

Like Mercedes often said, nobody sits in the car while others eat at the Hungry House. If you must

The Traveler

save your money for two months to go eat there, then do it.

Wide wood-framed glass windows were on all sides, and on the river beyond the glass, people were boating and casting nets. Laughter and loud squeals came from children trying to help dads toss seines into the river. Paradise.

Boaters waved as they sailed past the restaurant overlooking the river. This is just more of the Heaven which is the Georgia coastline. Shhh!

Malik smelled fresh shrimp frying, hush puppies, fish, oysters boiling. This was the kitchen to eat at he thought. And he knew because he had eaten there many times.

A few years had passed since he'd stopped here but it still looked and smelled the same. Great diners and restaurants never change, nor should they. They always smell like mama's kitchen.

Hanging on every wall were paintings of

African Americans in various headdresses and native clothing. Malike smiled and revived a few great memories.

A place in Nashville, Tennessee, where he often stopped when he was traveling through the world's music city, called *Shugga Hi*, where they boasted of eating dessert first, his motto, was a lot like this place.

In Nashville, the restaurant which served the best food in Tennessee, was decorated similarly.

Like at *Shugga Hi*, here at the Hungry House, gold framed paintings were done in oils, colorful rich textures and of African Americans with dramatic eyes and postures regal and decorated every wall. Bright beads had been added to a few of the canvasses, adorning headdresses, and bright clothing. Class and attitude here, like at *Shugga Hi* in Nashville, Tennessee. The food also was to die for. Best food in Georgia, right here and best food in Nashville, right there!

The Traveler

Malik was royal-related, so he accessed this outstanding artwork easily and with great joy.

Every painting had an attitude of cherished freedom and spirituality. He loved this place, and was already yearning for a visit to *Shugga Hi* in Nashville! Now he wanted those waffles at Shugga Hi, ha.

The atmosphere inside Hungry House at Shellman Bluff stirred a love of this culturally rich Southern area. The paintings and smells engulfed Malik who was thinking about two things, the mission before him, part of his heart and second, he thought about this:

In the amazing grace of Malik's last mile home, he immersed himself in memories of his "lost and found" times.

He remembered the long-ago pain of losing his best friend. He thought of how he'd been part of the crowd yelling No! No! And standing beside a tree, on a hill, Malik fell to the ground, overcome by many tears of such a torrent Malik thought he'd cried a river. He partly drowned.

This was part of the "lost" times. Or, as Malik thought, times of such loss no man can endure for long. Other losses: the time he'd lost a son and some people treated him coldly and pushed him away because they were too selfish to understand the pain of another human, especially a father. Or mother.

He remembered the shared pain and the disbelief. It was true, parents should not have to bury their blood children before themselves!

Many of them had never mourned children and did not understand Malik's heartbreak. Many of these fake friends were too narcissistic to allow Malik's attention to focus on grieving because that took the focus off them.

As Malik thought, he smiled at the ladies. lounging in their camo pants and black turtleneck shirts and black waders. They looked like Mafia or spies or close to it. Malik giggled and it came out hoarse, and he flashed a golden smile reminding Mercedes and Alona Lois of "their" ex-husband and best friend, as he was often referred to between the two of them.

Or plainly, "ours" and now here was the man – his twin!

They knew he was reading their minds. How was this? He knew they were wondering!

Don't ask me, ask life, he thought. He knew what they were thinking. Comparing him to Alona Lois's late husband--he was not--and to Mercedes's best friend, again, don't ask me, ask life. Ask the unknown, the supernatural. Ask what is a mystery? What if? Oh yeah, what if?

He leaned back, comfortable. His feelings were easy here at home here in the Hungry House Restaurant and he was hungry. He hoped the waitress whom he'd met before many years ago, didn't recognize him, lol, right.

He wore clean washed dark denim jeans with an open neck collar blue *Polo* shirt, tucked in, a belt with a tractor on the brass belt buckle, Wellington boots. He was tall and shoulders square. He beamed an honest smile from his amber, brown, hazel eyes (depending on the mood). His eyes changed color like one of those mood rings we used to wear.

Though his hair was the color of silver and wrinkles wink-winked at the corner of his eyes and along his jaw line, Malik exuded a peaceful, easy feeling only Southerners seem to possess. Classic, laid-back Southern attitude. Mr. cool.

The reason for this peaceful feeling among Southerners is they are, most often, at peace. A Southern gentleman true to his roots grows up learning from his daddy and his daddy's daddy before him, to be true to yourself and you'll be alright. Malik was full of confidence, and everyone saw it. One must be confident and full of courage to go on such a long, long journey. As an older man, his courage, however, seemed to be waning with every minute of every day!

Older is not easy, he often thought. And yes, folks are very surprised when they find their physical and mental acumen fading like a last of summer day. Nobody young understands what old means or is like. And everybody old is startled when they find out. Biggest surprise in life!

Malik looked a lot like Alona Lois's late husband. Who was enjoying (she said) his stay at a cemetery west of Augusta, Georgia. A man for all seasons Alona Lois declared, and how it pained her when he died, a few years ago.

Malik reminded Mercedes of the best friend she had lost! Who had indeed been Alona Lois's husband. Stranger things have happened! But the three of them loved one another beyond life.

Like a lost and found department, Malik's mind churned with different memories, all precious learning experiences in life. At the thoughts of these many memories, his heart felt both heavy and jubilant. Malik had made amazing memories and had taken many amazing journeys. Some people die young and some in infancy. He had been blessed with many miles!

Some live short lives but his was long indeed. Instead of one journey, like folks are in this life, Malik was chosen for many passings.

Malik was thankful to his Father in Heaven for choosing him to take these long journeys throughout the times of his life.

Time. As Malik aged time became precious. Like most of us, he counted the hours, and he made the hours count. No time for a sedentary life! If lazy folks knew what Malik knew about life beginning and ending at any time, short at the longest yard, they would get up off the
couch and make sure they made the most of their days. They would not waste an hour of their time!

So much to get done. So little time to do it. Malik had planned such an easy mission, or so it seemed in the planning stage. Go figure! Make plans and get ready for twists to the story....and Murphy's law kicking butt. Nothing goes as planned!

Action was required and he had planned to be on his way up to Savannah and then to TYBEE where he would launch this project. He had lucked into a great ride. Although he was no hitchhiker, he considered it good to ride with these ladies, in the red Ford F-150 truck with the gray cloth seats. He had once owned such a truck! He missed his truck!

Supposedly, this mission would begin quite soon, maybe after a night of rest in Savannah.
Then prayer and launch the calling which had been a dream of Malik's for what felt like forever. This was his plan. Perfect, or so it seemed.

Dreaming again, like we all do.

Summertime is a time of dreams.

He was brought back to reality by the appearance of the waitress who recited today's menu verbatim without looking at a menu. Her sing-song words flew through the gold front teeth like splattering sea foam through a net.

At the same time reality kicked him because little petite, excitable, dramatic, pretty good one, platinum blonde, Mercedes (always into something) had disappeared. He looked at her empty seat and knew two things. She was gone; that was one. And two, it meant trouble.

As he was going, "Hmmmm," while looking quizzically at Alona Lois who was also smiling but had crossed her arms, the waitress hurried to their table.

"She's gone to the lady's room," said Alona Lois. She turned both palms up and frowned.

"How long has she been gone?" asked Malik.

"Too long," declared Alona Lois. "I'll go see what's wrong."

At which time the waitress who had just dashed up, said breathlessly through the gold teeth, "Ya friend done fell in!"

"What?" said Malik, pushing back his chair.

"Wait," said Alona Lois, "I'll go. She's always doing stuff like this." And Alona Lois stood up from the chair and followed the waitress out of the dining area, down a long hall and stood before the door of the ladies' room, which was marked **CLOSED FOR CLEANING**.

"She in yonder," said the waitress, standing before the men's room door. She placed her hands on her hips, like I told ya so.

Alona Lois pushed open the door, taking a deep breath. With Mercedes, you never knew.

Through the small crack in the door, Alona Lois saw Mercedes getting up off the floor in stall no. 2. Stall no. 1 was empty.

The room was empty, but clearly a men's room. What in the world?

Mercedes brushed off her camo jeans, as she came through the very narrow stall door and put a finger to her lips, "Shhhhh. I've found something and reading it."

Alona Lois mouthed "What?"

"Shhhh...not here...."

Mercedes calmly walked to the faucets and washed her hands. She wiped them and pulled open the bathroom door. She took a deep breath.

"I told ya she fell in!" said the waitress.

"I didn't fall in, goodness," said Mercedes laughing. "I just saw the other bathroom was locked and I needed to go in there!

Nobody was in there and I dropped something on the floor. Looking for it!"

"Oh, Lort!" said the waitress walking off, shaking her head.

"Shhh," said Mercedes as they walked back into the dining room and to the table where Malik sat, smiling. He stood when they got to the table and pulled out their chairs.

"I found something and read something and my goodness, you need to know!" Said Mercedes.

Malik was staring at the other men in the room for suddenly he knew who they were: the U.S. Marshals from the Fugitive Task Force, who had chatted with him at Big Daddy Island, at the cabin, Yellow. They were looking for a fugitive which they said Malik resembled!

Coincidence, NOT! Malik thought. He was uneasy but not too. He smiled uneasily. He knew that he needed to figure this out before it went farther. Were those guys following him?

"Found?" said Malik. "Cell phone?"

"Tell us, come on!" said Alona Lois, leaning forward. "What did you find in there?"

"It has something to do with you," said Mercedes. She reached beneath her black shirt and pulled out a black I Phone with a message and a red light on. "Shhhh! I've already read the message and it scares me. I'm like astonished!"

"Whose cell phone?" whispered Alona Lois?

Mercedes nodded toward the men across the dining room, looking out at the river. So far, the men had not noticed Alona Lois, Mercedes, and Malik. Or at least it didn't seem so. No one saw them turn around, but some people, mothers for example, do have eyes in the backs of their heads. Maybe these men do!

"Well, let's see it, "said Malik. Although he knew what it said. Of course, part of his many strong suits was knowing beforehand.

Mercedes passed him the cell phone and said, "Shhhh..." again. She held her finger to her lips.

Alona Lois covered her mouth, eyes wide, and whispered, "Don't let the waitress see this."

"I won't," said Mercedes, crooking her neck and pretending to stare at a painting on the wall, of a woman with a headdress of white feathers.

The piano player was playing the old funky song, *My Girl*, and Malik felt sad. He read the message on the phone, his mind went blank, then corrected quickly. Go figure! He frowned.

Just like that, the mission changed.

Rather than go easy and smooth, launch at Tybee with ceremony, he was caught in launching the mission here and now.

Information on the U.S. Marshals phone told of an ugly danger to pets close by. Stolen, without a doubt. They needed him; er, them.

He was positive they saw Red and were fighting mad to go on this mission with him to save these precious pets. They did not know the dangers involved but they appeared tough but were they tough enough for this mission? He hoped so.

They were the types who hung on like bulldogs ya know, like 90-year-old toenails. How well Malik remembered Alona Lois, and Mercedes! Oh yes, his heartbeat raced! My girls. He smiled.

He felt burdened. He not only had a dangerous mission ahead, which of course, he was embarking upon immediately! But he didn't want the ladies to get hurt!

They were going with him. He couldn't stop fate. And didn't want to. Never had.

Malik knew to follow the process and not let his emotions dictate his action.

The food was brought, and they ate fast and enjoyed the amazing seafood. Malik said nothing, too busy planning the details before him.

They ate in silence as Malik handed the phone back to Mercedes who passed it beneath the table to Alona Lois who read the message and turned white, her mouth flying open and staying ajar as she read the message, astonished.

Wasting no time, the three stood up. Malik paid the check, and they walked out the door.

Behind them came the U.S. Marshals.

Malik could not stop them, nor help them and what they were about to do. Malik mumbled that his guess was not that good, but it did not matter.

He knew what they were fixing to do.

Being a Southern gentleman, he knew it and the women knew it, but having been born and raised in this life, in Savannah, Georgia to Godly parents, Malik felt pain in his soul. He felt a heaviness of heart. He covered his face with his big right hand as though shielding his amber gaze and wept loudly. He felt broken but also, mad.

Alona Lois felt sad about this entire situation. She felt tears and she never cried so this was new. It hurt her heart and she wasn't hard hearted, but she almost never cried. The tears grazed her cheeks and she felt relief. It's alright to cry, came to her, and she didn't bother to wipe the tears. Tears are good. They clean us up. She was ready for Malik's mission to save these pets.

Mercedes cried openly but not loudly. She sniffled as she watched Malik weep.

She had seen Big Daddy weep before, his heart so heavy she could feel it coming apart and her own heart hurt. This was just like that!

Alona Lois opened the driver's door, Mercedes got in on her side and Malik stopped weeping and said goodbye to the fawning waitress with her gold teeth shining. She stood on the porch and waved goodbye.

He offered an embarrassed, humble smile, stood, and turned around and climbed into the red truck.

Time to go. Like a man's man, Southern man, Simple but wise man, Malik was not a time waster. He was on the job and focused. Despite some fear and trepidation for the women.

His own clock was ticking, and this mission was too critical to delay. It was time. The Fur babies had only hours left to live. They had to get there before midnight!

When we feel called of God, we feel both joy and sorrow. Sometimes we fear we won't satisfy the world's expectations, but as soon as we realize we are hesitating, the thought disappears, and we fill up with the thrill of knowing we are following His great plans. Obedience gives comfort! Obedience fosters trust!

The happy in Jesus feeling kicks in, and we know without doubt, we are doing the Lord's work. The gospel will indeed, be published, presented, broadcast and emulated, inspired and appear in every move of our lives, such as Malik. Plans for this mission, although dangerous, had been laid out. They were ordered. Ordered by God.

On these amazing earth-changing God-sent missions, we follow in foreordained footsteps.

Malik wiped his still wet eyes with the back of his right hand and his chest swelled with pride.

Although old and fragile, more physically than mental, and less immune to the dangers and pain of a surprisingly cruel world, Malik felt courage seep into the seams of his soul.

He prayed, Father God, please send me courage. Don't let these two ladies lose it when this comes off, the big rescue.

Don't let them scream and holler and head for the hills. May we stay calm and do the job we've been sent to accomplish! He sat there quietly, his cup running over. His mission was so close he could smell it and touch it.

And after the mission was over, Malik would take his final last mile, happy to go, happy to be going home!

As he sat there in the truck, he sighed and planned. Alona Lois and Mercedes said nothing as Alona Lois cranked up and let the truck run for a few minutes and the ac come on good.

Malik was proud to be a brave Southern Gentleman. Being a Southern Gentleman was one of the classiest things a man could be. He enjoyed it. He had courage and manners…two in one!

Better than a man from any place on earth, Malik loved nature and was one with the creatures and the dirt, yes, the dirt. After all, he was clay.

He was flesh and bone and spirit created by a Heavenly Father! Wasn't he wrestling with the challenges of this mission, and wouldn't he not let this mission go before it blessed him!

Oh yes, and he felt the power of a Holier spirit more than ever before. It chilled him with self-respect and spiritual fuel for the mission.

He gave Alona Lois the address they needed to get to, and fast, and he felt pride rise within him. He was about to fight for the Lord! Battle!

And as he had thought many times before, launching a God-ordained mission:

I am the Traveler.

The man with wings.

Worlds without end.

Chapter 6:

The Mission

Malik, Alona Lois, and Mercedes sat in silence, in the parking lot of the Hungry House Restaurant and Alona Lois entered the information for the house they needed to find, into the Garmin.

Through the back window of the truck, which Malik had down, and like whispers on a summer breeze, the strains of funky *My Girl* played from the restaurant.

The jazz guitarist of course, livened it up and Malik thought once and forever, My Girls. These are the women of this journey, the ones who choose to go with me. He sighed and a smile softened his serious face. It was planned for sure, and not by Malik!

As Alona Lois backed out the truck and then pulled onto Highway 17, turning North, Malik looked back. He wished he was headed downcoast to Big Daddy Island, but he was not, and he never would go that way again. He sighed.

He was here on purpose, and you might say, at this age, repurpose. All three of them were here on repurpose, Malik thought, and felt this was clever. Repurpose. At their age, repurpose is about right.

Downcoast at Big Daddy Island was where his heart was. But north Georgia was where his heart was going. They had animals to rescue.

They were leaving the south part of Georgia headed north and would soon, in a few hours go west. They would be west and north of Savannah when they got to their destination.

Taking care of business, in the words of Elvis, and it felt good. Malik was ready to do this.

Malik thought that people don't get their ducks in a row, get their priorities straight. Many people just goof off day in and day out and never have anything to show for it.

Well, not him and not Alona Lois nor Mercedes. All three were hard workers, with homes and land to show for it.

God expects us to roll up our sleeves. We look forward to going to special places. Places in our hearts make our pulses race and our spirits are elevated and set upon pedestals of harmony and joy. We love vacations.

We talk about serving others but how many do we really serve? How many people have we given clothes to, taken food to sick houses, don't someone a favor, lately?

So called Christians talk about their good deeds but the ones who do things, don't normally talk.

Let God honk your horn, Malik always said.

We work and spend money on material things but not missions where we are called to serve. People work and slave and bend and torture their time until there is no more time to go to places where memories are laid in stone, with family and loved ones. With our pets.

Priorities. If God calls your name, please, ask what? What will you have me to do?

We are born of the Spirit and choose to come into a world of flesh and someday we'll leave the flesh behind like we found it and the spirit will return to its original intention. Soaring into the infinity of our inheritance from God the Father.

What are our marks on life? What good things are we leaving behind us when we go?

Malik loved the amazing gospel song, written by Carl Trivette in 1952 for his wife, Marilee Rasnake Trivette, *I Want to Stroll Over Heaven with You,* and Malik hummed it as he settled into the back seat.

Malik touched the stones he wore on a silver chain around his neck. They gave him comfort.

He was from a time and place these ladies would never understand until it was time to know and understand. Everything in its season, he thought and yet, the day would come that Malik would Stroll over Heaven with them. He liked the thought a lot. He would stroll over Heaven with them and with the fur babies of his life and they would stroll along with their fur babies.

God almighty, his Father in Heaven ordained it. It was not exactly going to be the easy mission he'd thought at first, but he was so fired up about rescuing these animals that a fire threatened to consume him, right there in the Ford F-150 truck. He remembered oddly how Alona Lois operated.

She was an excellent driver. She was older, he hoped it was still true. She was punctual and organized, unlike her sidekick Mercedes, creative and a drama queen! But both loved dearly!

So, this was his last mission, the last time with these ladies. The thought made him happy knowing he was making memories with them. Although the mission had changed and grown into a scary series of made for movies events.

As Alona Lois drove, Malik rolled up the window and closed his eyes. The restaurant was a few miles back and he could no longer smell the food or hear the music. He was leaving.

Tears sprang to his eyes, and he thought of the years he had spent ensconced in the love of Big Daddy Island.

He wanted to recall the wet dog smell of the rivers and Doboy Sound and the sting of salt water, boats, nets, cypress, loblolly pine needles. The fish smell. Sand on the feet smell. Driftwood and mud. Birds.

Sweat.

Malik leaned back against the gray seat and thought about missions. Every journey or project—mission, Malik dubbed it--we are called to by our loving Heavenly Father. Malik chose, of course, to accept his Father in Heaven's callings upon his life. He knew that our lives and steps are ordered, and our journeys orchestrated by God in Heaven.

Now if the mission is a God-called mission, every door will open, that No man can shut, and if it is not of GOD, no doors open or if they do, will shut in your face. If it is God the Father calling, and we answer, the way is not only possible, but made and laid in stone! A done deal!

If you call yourself and the project is not God ordained, the doors are locked against it. You can knock and knock triple, kick, shake, rattle, and batter the door and you can't open it. But oh my! If the mission is of God, supernatural power opens every door. Not to say all goes smoothly, it often does not, but it will go. And succeed!

As we age, we retire and think, well that's it for working. NO more work for me, I'm just going to spend the rest of my life sitting around and watching television. People who are older (Seniors) think we are too old to write and record music, take part in plays or movies, go on cruises, wear fun clothes; but no, we are not.

If we feel called of GOD to do something, do it! It's a win in the making.

People make the mistake of thinking they have all the time in the world to get something done.

The surprise is we don't know how much time we have left but we know time does not wait for us. It moves forward and never stops. We might stop but time does not.

We can't "take time" nor "stop time" nor beg borrow nor steal time. Time does its thing, and moves on. We can move along, accept our "new" calling or projects and make the "most" of the gift of time or waste it. One of the worst tragedies of life is wasted time.

Malik thought of the scripture he loved so much, about God making plans for us.

Now he was on the final mission as a person on earth, headed for victory, he knew. But it wouldn't be the easiest thing in the world.

"I know an animal control officer and we are going to stop and talk with him at Buddy Alman's store at the crossroads," said Mercedes.

"That might be a good idea," said Alona Lois.

"Ok," Malik agreed because agreeing was the smart thing to do. Plus, information is always good, he thought. Even though I do not need it, I don't think! However, the mission which had suddenly become an emergency mission, was imminent. Ready or not here Malik and Alona Lois and Mercedes came!

"Everybody doesn't love animals like we three people." Alona Lois thought out loud, driving the red truck smoothly,

"True," said Mercedes, "but I do. And nobody is going to harm one on my watch!"

"You and me both," said Alona Lois. "I can't stand the thought of cruelty to animals!"

Malik thought of the message on the U.S. Marshals cellphone, and it was earth shattering and almost unbelievable. Nothing surprised Malik but he was sure these ladies were about to get an eye full. He had seen some bad things during his years wandering all over this planet but nothing as bad as this.

Malik had stood alone in a far place and watched friends killed on crosses, one time a woman burned at the stake for being a witch when everybody knew she was a servant of God.

Malik had lived and often borne witness to the sad truth of a world full of meanness, toward people and animals, kids, the earth itself. He was no stranger to cruelty to men or animals. He was no stranger to trouble and the demons of hell devouring innocent souls of living creatures of all stripes. He knew all about "whom he may," and people living like the devil and being eaten up by demons that troll the earth for victims.

Now, this great mission before them would be nasty in many ways. From information on the found cell phone, the pair of U.S. Marshals from the Fugitive Task Force were tailing Malik to back up local law enforcement who were staking out, investigating an old house on Lovely Lavender Lane, located northwest of Savannah, Georgia.

And arrest a cult leader. Witches! Bad witches! An informant who had left a cult, had blown the whistle on the witch coven.

Reader, you may think such is not true, but it is. It didn't make the newspaper, but it should have. The U.S. Marshals said so, and I say so.

"How long will this trip take?" asked Mercedes.

"With a few stops, not that bad. We need to get out and stretch our legs, I know I do," said Alona Lois.

"I have to stretch mine," said Malik.

"I have to walk around a bit," said Alona Lois, "And I'll be fine."

"Well, if we stop at that store, then go on, be a few hours is all." Alona Lois drove on.

"This won't make the news, but we will save and free the animals. The law enforcement agents will bust this horrible, mean party up."

They were headed for an old house a few miles to the North side and west of Savannah where 100 fur babies were trapped in kennels and cages of various sizes. The precious, stolen fur babies were going to be used as live sacrifices by a Witch's coven. The witch coven was staked out by the GBI, FBI and the U.S. Marshals Service.

The bust might be another Waco, it appeared, and Malik and the ladies were going to save the animals before the fires started! They had no choice! It was do or die trying!

Malik was being tailed by the U.S. Marshals Fugitive service because he resembled a fugitive from justice listed on their top ten wanted list. He appeared to be a foreigner, although Malik had told them in plain English he was born and raised in the good 'ole U.S. of A.   He didn't look Southern, but he acted southern, because in this story, in this second act of a three-act play, suitable for a horror movie, Malik was southern born and bred. His parents were immigrants.

In this story, his mother had been a dark-haired Jewish born lady and his father dark haired and kept his hair slicked back, old movie star style. Malik's beautiful mother was named Yva and his father was named Nematta. They had lived out their lives owning a successful company, a distributor of specialty goods to local stores, in Savannah, Georgia and throughout Georgia.

Malik attended local schools. Played sports and enjoyed a good and Godly upbringing. However, his mama had loved gospel music and frequented often, a Southern Baptist church where they sang loud and lively. And the preacher yelled.

Malik loved this music, and especially loved soul music and blues. Like other teens, Malik had a guitar and some tambourines and now and then talked his friends into playing music in the garage with the idea of forming their own band.

So, Malik had grown up Southern, all the while knowing his true beginnings and knowing his purpose in life from day one.

He was called and he knew it.

His mother told him so and his father agreed.

There were no siblings, but Malik was surrounded by pets of all kinds. His mother and father believed they were preparing Malik to spend his life working with animals as a veterinarian.

But his mother and father passed away two years before he finished college and Malik focused on this mission and moving forward to join them.

He ran his daddy's company, made a good

living, lived a good life, and grew older. His mission was always on his mind. He had thought at one time he had missed the opportunity to complete the mission and now, in old age, here it was. He was here, he was doing it.

He had collected the necessary stones to bring along with him, for protection, prosperity for the journey and supernatural energy.

He knew his mission and his mission had known him since, well, before the world was. He had planned and reviewed and embellished the mission for many years now. Now it was on.

The chase was on. The mission before him, although yes, a few twists and turns had already occurred. There would be more, he imagined.

While the mission wasn't going as he had planned, smooth, it was going.

Malik smiled.

"What in the world are you thinking?" asked Mercedes, stretching her neck around the front passenger seat. He had been quiet for a while.

Alona Lois laughed. She was wondering the same thing!

Malike giggled hoarsely. He knew they would like to pick his brains! He would explain some of it. But not that much. They already knew too much!

"This mission has been with me for a long time," he said. "I just had no idea it would work out this way, riding up the highway along the Georgia coast with you two old women."

"Watch what you call us," Mercedes laughed.

"We are old enough to know better but crazy enough to do it anyway!" said Alona Lois.

Alona Lois slowed down and turned left into a parking lot at a store, wooden sides, a long porch-another porch with rocking chairs--and a tin roof. The print on the side of the building said, "Buddy Store" and beneath: Former Animal Control Officer, tales and cheap beer sold inside.

Alona Lois said, "This is the animal control officer. He is a former policeman, and I want to talk to him about our project! Won't tale 15 minutes."

"That's right," Mercedes said, eyes wide.

"Ok," said Malik. The ladies thought they were helping him in the action ahead. He liked information although he didn't need it.

Alona Lois got down from the truck, as did Mercedes on her side and Malik from the second truck door.

Buddy himself opened the store door and welcomed them inside. There were no cars or trucks in the parking lot and Buddy stood at the bar knocking back a Coke.

"Y'all want a beer, I'm out till the truck comes later on this afternoon," asked Buddy. He shrugged his shoulders. Buddy wore a t-shirt with guns crossed on the front, and jeans. He was clean and neat and stood straight and just under six feet tall. He had old blonde hair, and a receding hair line and a stub of a ponytail. Buddy Allman was not one of "the" Allman's but liked everybody to believe he was. Pictures of famous bands hung on the wall behind the bar. In the center was the Allman Bros band, a group photo.

"We'll sit at the counter and just chat a bit, about animals, or anything else," said Alona Lois.

"Oh hi, Miss Alona Lois, just now recognized you, that get-up threw me off a little."

Alona Lois laughed. She stopped here often, for gas and supplies. She was surprised he had not recognized her and knew it was because they

Did appear odd in black, long sleeve turtleneck shirts and camo jeans, plus waders. Alona Lois also wore a t-shirt with a golf cart. Mercedes wore a shawl over her shoulders.

She smiled. This was July and hot. Good grief!

They were old ladies for lands sakes! Normally Alona Lois and Mercedes wore shorts, tee shirts, and tennis shoes.

Alona Lois, Mercedes, and Malik crawled onto bar stools, hard as bricks, and sat. All ordered Cokes while they twisted to get comfortable.

"I wanted to know, and I knew you would know, if we needed approval to go onto someone's property and maybe rescue a dog, or cat?"

"Oh now, you mean trespass?" said Buddy and stopped drying drinking glasses. He leaned on the counter and narrowed his eyes.

"I went on a property once, trespassed and I

knew it, and rescued or thought I was rescuing a lizard," Buddy said, laughing loudly.

"Everybody in that neighborhood called the cops and they called me, animal control. They swore a big lizard was on the loose and had them all terrified! Everybody locked their doors," Buddy said, and laughed and slapped his hip.

"Turns out it was a pet lizard, alright, a toy some little girl had thrown out the car window and the dogs carried it all over the place, barking.

Somebody reported it was one of them South American monster lizards and everybody had their doors shut tight and their guns loaded."

Everybody laughed.

"Nobody cared if I was trespassing or not, that time!"

"I'm sure!" grunted Mercedes. "But we want to know if we three here," she pointed to Alona

Lois and Malik, if WE go onto some property, do we need what a warrant, or what do we need."

"Well, y'all it depends on what's going down really." Buddy opened another beer.

"That's right and how dangerous and crazy," said Mercedes. "Never heard anything like it!"

"Well, the smart thing is it depends on whose property and if they are home or not," laughed Buddy.

"I'll take a hotdog," said Malik, eyeing the hotdogs in a glass oven, "all the trimmings."

Mercedes looked at Alona Lois, "Let's get one, we might not get to eat for a long while tonight!"

Alona Lois knew her stomach wouldn't like it one bit, but said, "Yes, I want one." To heck with the diet, eat what you want!

"Do you folks, Miss Alona Lois, and friends,"

started Buddy and offered a big smile. He reached up and turned his Braves baseball cap around backwards. "By some chance, do you know of an animal situation I need to know about. Or call an authority?" His smile became a glare!

"No!" said Malik quickly. He already had enough help with the ladies here.

Plus, they were all about to devour delicious smelling hotdogs. But the truth was they were all full and just *thought* they were hungry. Maybe, save them for later?

The ladies looked at Malik and realized this was so serious they didn't need to let the cat out of the bag! Whoops!

"My coke tastes flat, is that old Coke or what?"

"The Coke is fresh!"

"No, it's not," said Mercedes now laughing.

Alona Lois said, "Mine tastes fine."

"Here, taste mine," said Mercedes sliding her glass toward her friend. Alona Lois lifted the glass and drank some. It was flat, awful! Tasted very old. And didn't taste like Coke at all. In fact, it tasted like what? Nasty!

"It is flat honey, and can you get her another one?" Alona Lois said. "Hers tastes like beer?"

"Mine is flat too. I hate to tell you," Malik said. "Now, it's alright. No harm done."

Buddy said, "The Cokes aren't flat and no, I'm not getting anybody another one. I don't sell flat Cokes."

"Gross! Taste this," said Mercedes, handing her glass to Buddy who sniffed the drink, then tossed the drink down the drain behind him. He was red in the face when he turned around.

"Girl, ya drinking beer!" said Buddy.

Mercedes gagged.

Alona Lois gagged. "Goodness," she exclaimed! "How did this happen? Mercedes hates beer! Makes her puke!" Alona Lois brushed off her camo jeans and adjusted her black turtleneck shirt.

"Y'all are dressed uh, different today," said Buddy. "Used to see you ladies in Bermudas or denim jeans!" Trying to change the subject.

He kept going, "I was the law once and I smell a rat!" He wondered what Alona Lois, Mercedes and Malik were up to concerning an animal rescue. Buddy wanted to know if it was around here or not.

Buddy hated people who abused or ignored caring for their pets.

If the ladies and their companion had something up those long black sleeves, then he might be able to help them. If it had to do with animals of any description. He had experience, plus he loved animals, simple as that.

Malik said, finishing off his hotdog and wiping his big hands on a brown napkin, "We have to go now, thank you!" He stood up off the bar stool.

"I want a refund for the drink I thought was a Coke," Mercedes said, standing beside the bar stool. "In fact, I probably want refunds for the entire set of drinks and the hotdogs. The nerve of you serving us beer when we asked for Coke!" She laughed but it wasn't funny to Buddy Alman.

"No, that's alright," said Alona Lois turning to Buddy, still standing there with his arms crossed behind the bar, Braves baseball cap on backwards.

"No. I'll give shorty a refund but not you other two, nothing was wrong with y'alls, right?"

"Right!" said Alona Lois. "Kinda."

"Well okay, let's go," said Malik, paying the bill. He rubbed his arm and started walking toward the door.

"And are you headed to rescue an animal of some sort, is my question?" said Buddy.

"All I want is a refund."

"It was only a dollar," said Malik. "I'll give you a dollar, let's go!"

"I'm not moving a step till this man refunds me! I am a Christian and honest to the nth and I'm not trying to be rude, just standing up for my rights!"

"Look, it's no big deal, he made a mistake!" said Alona Lois. She formed a shhhh on her lips.

"No big deal to you, I was the one drinking that mess!" said Mercedes. "And I feel sick!"

Now she was fuming at such shoddy service. "He also called me "Shorty" and I am offended by it," said Mercedes. "I can't help my size." Mercedes was a Senior Citizen but didn't look it, and she thought of herself as Queen of everything. Her cowgirl attitude didn't take many prisoners! She felt this man disrespectful and making fun now of her height, 5'3", standing beside Alona Lois's 5'6".

Malik was at least 6' 1" tall which made Mercedes feel even more sawed off. She was sensitive about her height! People have feelings.

"No, y'all just can't go on other people's property to rescue animals and no, you can't break into anyone's house. If you suspect an animal is being abused or mistreated, call the law. Animal Control officers will come!"

"We know animal control officers. We have a good-looking one in our town and he's a lover of animals and he knows the law. We'll call him if we need advice," said Alona Lois as she walked out the door and headed for the red truck. She couldn't get there fast enough. She had to get Mercedes away from Buddy who seemed in a crazy smart aleck mood today! He was barking up the wrong tree!

Mercedes said loudly, "I want my REFUND," a mantra. "I want my refund!"

Buddy ran down the steps behind them and handed Mercedes two one-dollar bills. "I'm sorry, I don't need a fight with a customer."

"You won't win with me. What don't kill me better start running!" She said and took the bills from Buddy. "We don't want a fight either but that was bad stuff you handed me! Just because I am a Christian don't mean I'm a chicken."

Alona Lois said, "We'll just pray about this and see you another time, no harm done!" Alona Lois knew Buddy and he'd always been nice before, but then again, he had never handed them a beer either, disguised as Coke. Ugh!

Standing beside the red truck, they felt more at ease and that the Coke, beer incident was a small thing. The art of letting things slide was a good art to know, thought Malik.

"Yes, no harm," said Malik, a peace lover bar none, and the three crawled back into the red Ford F-150 and Alona Lois cranked it up and headed out of the parking lot and North up SR99.

The idea of going to a witch's coven, who ever dreamed anything like this could even exist? It was horrifying but they weren't about to back out! Too late now.

This is what Alona Lois was thinking as she drove, listening, not saying anything. Getting nervous. It was alright to be afraid. She had never been one to scare easily. But it was alright if she did!

"How far is it to this lace we are going to do the rescue?" Mercedes asked.

"Well, an hour and a half maybe," according to this Garmin.

Alona Lois said, "I'm ready to get it over with!" She was headed north and then west. They were really going to do this! Her skin had goosebumps.

"Yes, and Alona Lois has a gun and I have a pistol and I know how to use it," said Mercedes.

"Have you ever used it?" Malik asked.

"Well, haha, not really. Maybe killed a few snakes with it," said Mercedes. "I never loaded the pistol myself. A cousin helped me, and I shot it one time or two. I don't like guns!"

"That's what I thought," said Malik.

"Well, this is not that far so we need to plan out how we'll go in and get the animals. We can't just knock on the door and run in screaming and grabbing animals. Someone might be in there!"

Malik added, "Plus we are all three Senior Citizens. I don't know about you girls, but I'm about as beat up as I can get. I've never been so tired in my life!" he sighed deeply.

"Don't worry you will have energy when we need it! I'm tired too and stay that way a lot. No spring chickens here," said Mercedes.

Alona Lois laughed. "I'm tired too! 40 years of driving a mail route car will kill a person!" I'm shook, rattled, and rolled from all those red dirt bumpy backroads on my route!"

She continued, "This is a wild and rather crazy idea but I'm in it to my eyeballs. I normally don't do unusual stuff and nothing involving danger, ha. I will not call my daughters. They'd have a fit and order me home. Very protective of me after their father died."

"Oh Lord. Mother Mary help us on this mission…." Said Mercedes.

"You're not Catholic!" said Alona Lois, laughing.

"I might be before this is over!"

The three of them laughed and then fell silent. Not a sound inside the big red Ford F-150 except the whirring of the truck motor and the slapping of tires on the two-lane asphalt.

And this was the point at which the three started crying. Unusual, yes. But the excitement and the fear combined was simple too much. A good cry is not easy but somehow, helps!

Mercedes cried loudly. "Don't mind me, I get caught up excited. I cry when I'm mad and I cry when I'm glad. I guess the danger is worrying me. I'm a nervous wreck!"

"I just love animals and the thought of someone stealing another family's fur baby is horrible. It's…it's EVIL is what it is!" Mercedes coughed. "God don't like it!" She wiped her eyes with a handkerchief and said, "I'll rescue and tote my end of the weight."

"As I will mine!" chimed Alona Lois. "We've been in situations like this before, and it took a lot of praying to get out of."

"So right, when the boat capsized near Sapelo Island when we were having our summer retreat at Big Daddy Island!"

"Five of us on the boat! Boat sunk and us on it, in a storm!" said Alona Lois. I still have nightmares about it."

"God saved us from drowning!"

"I remember it," said Malik softly but Alona Lois nor Mercedes heard him, so caught up they Were, in remembering this horrifying near miss tale.

"Anyhow, everybody knows I grew up on a farm near the Satilla River, and with all types of animals. I always had kittens and dogs. Daddy loved German Shepherds, so my first dog was a German Shepherd, Rusty."

"I grew up with them too, we always had yard dogs, not so many cats around but chickens for sure. My daddy farmed a lot and was a painter," said Alona Lois. "I had a sister who is dead. I also have a brother, not well, but I am caring for him! Whew! It's a job!"

"Well, this might be dangerous, so we need to plan it out and talk about how we are going to get into this house on *Lovely Lavender Lane.*"

"That is correct…and I've got *Lovely Lavender Lane* in the Garmin, a few road curves and twists and turns and we'll be there."

"It is after 3:00 o'clock in the afternoon so when we get there it will be around maybe 5-6 once we find the place," said Malik from the back seat.

"I'd guess around five," said Alona Lois, driving the red Ford F-150 smooth as sailing on a ship with the wind at its back.

"Y'all try and get some rest," said Alona Lois, "I'm okay." Which she was not, she was too sleepy to admit.

Shortly, the only sound in the truck was Malik's heavy breathing. He had fallen asleep!

"I thought he was going to tell us what to do?" said Mercedes. "But she was half asleep too and just leaned back and that was it."

"He is," said Alona Lois.

The Traveler

"I am," whispered Malik.

"And me too," whispered Mercedes.

Chapter 7:

The Highway (SR 99)

Highway 99 or SR99 as it is known, runs along the Georgia coast from an intersection at Sterling, Georgia, for 38.9 miles to just past Fancy Creek south of Savannah, Georgia.

It is a two-lane road which, if you travel this highway through a little-known paradise called the Georgia coast you never forget it. Never in this life can you forget this piece of forever, out of time. The trip leaves you with a feeling of love for a place that will always live in your heart.

On this July morning, in the summer of '23, three friends, Alona Lois driving, Mercedes riding shotgun and "helping drive" and Malik snoring, in the back seat, were headed to a small town a short distance to the North and West of Savannah, called Ringgold, Georgia which was the starting point for Ebeneezer Creek. This creek, which is a kayaking paradise, runs downhill (of course) and is a tributary of the Savannah River.

Along the banks of the tall pines and live-oaks, tupelo trees and fanning palmetto bushes, are scattered houses, fishing shacks and a few cottages.

And along these creek banks about 20 miles from Savannah, Georgia, is a curvy drive, overgrown, narrow in spots, almost too narrow for a vehicle to slide through. Spooky.

This road was called Lovely Lavender Lane. And on *Lovely Lavender Lane* three lives were about to change forever. Alona Lois, Mercedes, and Malik were about to accomplish a daring and dangerous mission created by Malikhan Sharon.

Neither woman knew too much about him, but they wished to know more. Especially now!

The closer they got to Ringgold, Georgia, and time to stop and refuel, get Cokes, the more Alona Lois and Mercedes realized this adventure was different from their other sometimes hair brained schemes, which were a lot safer!

They chatted at the gas pump. Of course, Malik had gotten out of the truck and was pumping the gas. Southern gentleman, just like someone they had known and known well, once upon a time.

"We are doing a crazy thing," Alona Lois, said loudly. "Shows how bored to tears I stay!" She looked straight at Malik. "You do know how crazy this all sounds. And dangerous?"

"Yes, crazy!" said Mercedes.

"No, that's you, not me!"

"I know and I love it," said Mercedes.

"I know you do, but do we know what we are doing?" asked Alona Lois. "One of my girls just called and said, 'Mama you need to come home,' and I said, "I know,' and told them I'd call them back after-while. I told them Mercedes and I were rambling."

"Did you say, 'Honey is there an emergency?'" asked Mercedes. She knew and adored Alona Lois's daughters and four grandchildren. Class!

They laughed. They were Seniors and their children worried over them often telling them they didn't want them pulling crazy stunts.

The two daughters were determined to "raise their mother" right! Like Mercedes's son and his wife were.

Alona Lois's girls considered their mother a best friend, which was a blessing, and mature. But they did keep a check on her, which was good.

So did her growing grandchildren.

"Well, gas tank full," said Alona Lois, standing aside as Malik lifted the nozzle and replaced it at the pump. He brushed off his hands and grabbed a windshield brush from a tank beside the pump and began washing the windshield.

Which reminded them of another man who had once if the truth were known, owned this red Ford F-150. And always washed the windshield.

Malik listened to the women laugh and move around him and he thought sometimes he felt like Einstein and sometimes he felt like his brain was the size of a BB rolling down a four-lane highway, dumb, dumb. These ladies were smart.

And somehow on this God ordained final mission in life, a twist had occurred: two women, named Alona Lois, which had been the name of his wife in the real world, and Mercedes, a best friend in the real world, showed up and fell into the project with him.

Malik knew the two ladies also found him very familiar, because, well, er, maybe he was familiar!

He smiled at the thought as the ladies came back out of the minute market with cokes and candy bars, chips for all three. They loaded the truck and Alona Lois cranked up and pulled out onto the highway.

They had left SR 99 for a while to go by Shellman Bluff and eat at the Hungry House Restaurant, (Highway 17) but soon got back on this road to go north. Now they were headed along some winding roads, north and west, trying to find Ringold, Georgia. They drove up backroads north, west, and back east of Ringgold, Georgia. At last, a few hours later, they saw a bronze marker: Ebenezer Creek.

Ebenezer Creek wound down and around through old growth Cypress and tupelo forests, and is a tributary of the Savannah River. You've never seen such a sight of large Cypress knees and wildflowers and majestic sprawling black water swamps. Georgia is famous for nature and nature honors the claim.

Malik touched the silver cross on the chain around his neck and next to his heart. On the chain were also, the precious, protecting jade, which gave him energy and other stones for direction and light.

"I am a writer. I want permission from both of you to write down the details of what we are doing. Ok?" asked Mercedes, writing in her notebook.

"Sure, write it. Make a good one!" said Alona Lois, turning to the right onto a two-lane road with another marker announcing *Ebenezer Creek-- Historic Site.*

"Thank you," said Mercedes. "Here it is!"

"Depends on what you are writing," laughed Malik. "And yes, we're almost to the house."

"My work is what is called, narrative fiction of a historical nature, which means what I tell that is true is true, but also, using the world FICTION, means some fiction of the story might be stretched a little bit. I like to make stuff up!"

"Yes, good," said Malik. He was looking at his cell phone and studying the location they were looking for. They were very close. He felt chilled and bumps raised on his hairy arms.

"We are going to drive to within a few hundred feet of the house and then get out and walk in. Stay behind me. Alona Lois has a gun, right?" Malik leaned forward as he instructed the ladies. He sounded hoarse like a youth.

He was quiet, almost whispering and very serious. God had prepared him for this this final mission to save animals, every animal he could! He was excited and at the same time, wary.

Both ladies thought, oh so familiar, that sound! They both realized they were about to lose it with Malik reminding them of we all know who.

"Right," said Alona Lois.

"Right," added Mercedes. She jotted a few notes and laid down the notebook and pen. "And I too have a jade stone, on a silver chain around my neck!" Whoa! She had forgotten to mention this!

Malik almost swallowed his tongue. He said nothing and continued studying the map on his cell phone.

"Might be strange, but I wear a jade on a silver chain around my neck. A gift from Mercedes!"

"Nothing strange at all about stones. If you collect stones or minerals, people might call you a little cuckoo but don't worry about that. I've always been a rockhound." Malik smiled.

He added, "Why…in the days of…." And he caught himself and fell silent.

The growth of cypress swamps increased and on either side of the narrow two-lane road headed east once again, the sun began to nosedive into the black waters of Ebenezer Creek.

"Who has been here before?" asked Malik, "Other than me?"

"Me," said Alona Lois. "One of the grandsons did a project on the eco-system of Ebenezer Creek and the historic value of the area; made an A Plus!"

"I've never been in this area, but I have heard of Ebenezer Creek and the horrifying disaster which occurred in the Civil War?"

"Yes, when the Union Leader pulled up the pontoon bridge, the one he'd built for his army to cross. A lot of innocent slaves died."

"Around 4,000, in the report by Grandson," said Alona Lois. "How horrible is this?"

"There are markers in case anyone wants to visit," Malik added.

"Yeah, we just passed that big bronze one," said Alona Lois.

"Keep driving, we don't have time to stop, and sight see; not now!" said Malik.

The truck moved along the two-lane road, going east now. Savannah, Georgia was 25 or so miles to the east. Ebenezer Creek was a tributary so followed the path downhill and east toward the coast.

Mercedes thought out loud, "Hmmm, if we are on Jekyll Island and maybe let's say, Driftwood Beach, sometimes stunning morning sunrises are making me think, beautiful blue eyes, or maybe pretty in pink, I mean, how can it get more beautiful?"

"I love Driftwood Beach, really everything about Jekyll, also Saint Simons Island. All the other barrier islands we used to go to in our boat,"

Alona Lois said.

"But I can tell you —and I do too, love the coast, especially Big Daddy Island," said Malik and giggled hoarsely. "But I can tell you…" he said, looking at Mercedes from the back seat of the Ford F-150, "This here is different."

"Ebenezer Creek is one of the last old growth bald cypress swamps in this world," said Alona Lois. "My grandson researched it!"

"It is scary," said Mercedes, but where is the house?"

"And I know, because I helped the grandson do his project, it is like stepping into a movie about prehistoric times."

"Did you paddle?" Asked Mercedes.

"Yes, we did!"

"It's either smoke (fog) and mirrors at early morning teeming with all sorts of life common to the eco-system, or late in the afternoon, which is scary I admit, beauties and beasts…beasts being those huge—I mean giant—bulbous looking tree trunks digging down into the dark water like claws on a monster!"

"I can imagine. It scares me just thinking about it!"

"You'd love it if you ever took a kayak down to the Savannah River," said Malik. "I haven't done anything like kayaking in many years, but I used to love it. I loved boats more." he faded.

"It's like being in another world, in fact a world class kayaking dream come true. They come here from all over the world," said Alona Lois.

Alona Lois drove the truck slower and slower. They approached a landing to the right, maybe a mile or so back in there toward the edge of the swamp.

Malik leaned forward between the two front seats and said, "Take a right and let's park at the landing and give the guys behind us a chance to go on down the rodeo!"

Alona Lois flipped the truck blinker to the right and the lights began flashing.

In the last hour, darkness had settled upon them. The night was becoming darker and darker. There were few lights, almost none, so yeah, dark.

An experience all three had enjoyed many times in the past and secretly wished they were there instead of here. Some stars up above, thank God.

But here was Malikhan Sharon's mission.

Here was what he believed in and felt God-sent and Glory-bound to complete. The mission. The stopping by to leave a mark on mankind, a heartfelt mission and a project of the soul.

Malik knew only that the U.S. Marshals who had been following them for hours now, up Highway (SR) 99 and veering left at Fancy Creek and then right and then curves galore and here they were. He knew they were close. Watching like they do.

The red Ford F-150 had passed Rincon, Georgia, and Alona Lois, drove past one of the most historic buildings in the U.S., Jerusalem Church, ast the *Ebenezer Creek Historical Marker* and along the two-lane road east following this historic trail.

The road swept and turned and laid down parallel to the creek, all the way to where it connected to the Savannah River.

Alona Lois pulled big Red into the parking spot, gravel crunching. They were the only truck out there except for an older Jeep with an empty boat-trailer behind it. Nobody in sight.

They could see the highway from where they were parked, and the headlights of a black SUV eased by, kept going. You know who.

"There they go," said Malik, laughing. "I don't mean to laugh, it's not funny at all."

In the crawling darkness of the Georgia hills and nearby swamp land of the creek, Malik thought of the word Ebenezer itself, which means in the Hebrew: *Stone of Help.*

"Feel of your jades," he said to the air and meant it. Alona Lois and Mercedes lifted their right hands and caressed the jades which hung on the silver chains around their necks.

Alona Lois said in a low voice—because it was dark, and eerie, strange and a lot getting scary. "Not meaning to be a wimp, but how much farther is it to this house we are going to? And how do we know who will be there?"

"We don't know ladies. But we are going to find out," said Malik. "We are on the job!"

"Will witches be there?" asked Mercedes.

"They might," said Malik. "We will stalk it out and it will be dangerous. I'm used to living on the edge and have faced danger before. Not sure you two have faced much danger."

"No, not really but I've endured a lot of pain. I lost a son and I'll never be the same, plus a husband that looked a lot like you!" said Alona Lois. She wanted to get this done and go home!

"And I lost both parents and a best friend," said Mercedes looking sideways at Alona Lois and reaching for her hand. "Who looked like Malik's twin brother!"

They fell silent, each thinking deep thoughts and with the window down, the sounds of crickets chirping (rubbing their wings together is how they "sing") and a male alligator somewhere off in swampy Ebenezer Creek bellowed, and the ladies jumped. Dang gator!

Malik smiled. "Mating season."

"Well supposedly it ends around June and his is starting July," said Alona Lois. She was up on this area history since the grandson had researched with her as assistant!

The night around them fell heavier like a black tarp and made them sleepy. They had been up since early and had left Big Daddy Island before lunch, then a few stops and hours on the road, they were pretty worn out.

Good conditions for remembering.

The air buzzed with mosquitos and Mercedes raised her window. Mosquitos in Georgia are jokingly referred to as giant birds with swords, so no invitations to being bitten.

July means heat in Georgia. While the coast at the Golden Isles is paradise, with those famous sifted sands and gentle breezes, blue skies, and sunsets pink and gold as melted crayons the land around Ebenezer Creek sprawled out under black waters and monstrous trees. Giant cypresses with knees and knobs and arthritic joints clawing beneath the surface, a movie set for a horror movie.

The quiet old world of the bald cypress swamp crawling along Ebenezer Creek (Stone of Help) reminded Malik of adventures when understanding the behavior of humans was beyond him. Beyond any creature created by a loving, kind Father in Heaven.

Where does the evil fit in, except of Satan devouring whom and what he may. His thoughts of the meanness of human beings, of the evil awaiting them in a house nearby, gave him a headache. He rubbed his temple.

He had not wanted to bring these two women into danger, perhaps violence, but life altered plans. God does not change HIS plans for us, but circumstances change plans!

Malik remembered pets and animals he'd loved during his journeys and throughout time his love for animals had grown. Sometimes, he knew deep down, the love of animals was deeper and more faithful than the love of humans.

A devoted animal will never forsake the person they love. A human will leave you for greener grass in the neighbor's yard. Not an animal.

A couple will pledge their devotion and faithfulness to a marriage and say, "Till death do we part," but many times what they mean is "Till death do we Party!" Empty words. Malik had seen it plenty of times. Fickle people.

Not so with animals who love and are bonded to you forever. There is simply no love as strong as that of a fur baby. Precious enduring bonds.

Malik had always shared life with animals. He loved them as companions. Once, he'd herded sheep, and that is another story known only to him, but yes, a sheep dog. Devoted to the end. He would never forget the sheep dog that lived with him for 15 great years.

Malik had been given a puppy once, a border collie when he was working with cattle out west. The border collie had saved Malik's life when cattle stampeded. To this night, Malik could close his eyes and hear the stampede and droning of wild cattle on the plains, him standing there in the path of destruction. Out of nowhere the collie had come running and turned the herd away.

Devotion. Animals are devoted. All they ask for is love and food. A warm place to sleep and kind words and they come to love their name and the sound of your voice. Calling them, talking to them.

What mercy and grace are given to a human being when a creature great or small, created by a loving **GOD**, comes into our lives. What love!

Malik breathed deeply. He had lived on that kind of love when humans had let him down, harmed him, harmed his best friend who was doing no harm, simply trying to change the world.

Malik smiled. Always a fur baby.

How this mission before him had changed to this job here, he did not know except that **GOD** steps in when a person cannot handle things.

Malik had never dreamed these two women would be with him tonight. It was nice, he thought, like a family get together in essence!

The dark shade of night along Ebenezer creek grew deeper, and Malik's thoughts fled him, and he snored lightly.

Alona Lois was startled.

The gentle snoring in the second seat sounded like **Big Daddy** snoring. Not a loud snore, but soft like a baby might snore when sleeping deeply.

Alona Lois glanced over at Mercedes. At least she had her best friend with her on this wild trip. At least she had her gun and knew how to use it. According to her faith, she would act. According to her goodness, she would do all she could to save the animals in question. Could be more than one, or a small or large number? She did not know but they would save them all. Her truck would haul, and she planned to load up what she could grab.

Alona Lois hated cruelty to animals in all forms.

In other countries they sold them in markets for food, and such evil gave her chills. In countries where they used them in lab trials (the U.S. included) and nothing short of torture, when did this nation get so far gone as to think cruelty to any living thing was okay?

Alona Lois was okay so far. She was not easily frightened, and she liked this man, Malik, in the back seat and that was okay too. At least he reminded her of the love of her life, Big Daddy. At least he had solid southern manners and knew how to act in public!

Her thoughts turned to the son she had lost.

A person does not know pain until they lose a child, no matter how old. They had a friend who also had lost a son to Covid a few years back and to this day, Alona Lois worried this great man would never overcome the loss. He had been married to a heartless witchy acting woman who never grasped the depth of his pain. He had divorced her and said it felt like throwing a rock stuck to you, as far as he could.

Anyhow, pain, yes, she had known pain. And no animal in her sight would know pain if she could help it.

The night was thick with wild noises and deep stillness. It gave her the creeps, but she was ready for whatever. She was ready to get the show on the road so she could go home.

Mercedes was startled by the sound of the big gator, which sounded a lot like an angry cow. "What's that?" There it was again.

"Well, gator, the same one," said Alona Lois.

"I was thinking of times gone by. We may be too old for this kind of stuff," Mercedes said.

"You chicken?" said Alona Lois.

"No ma'am, and you know better. I am tired is all." Mercedes hugged the shawl to her.

"I am too but we'll go shortly and see what's in the house," said Alona Lois. She cranked up the truck and it purred smoothly. "Maybe he'll wake up!"

And Malik did wake up. And he asked for prayers for the three of them and then he said, "My Father in Heaven planned this and is using us as his workers on earth. By his mercy and protection, we will succeed!"

"We like you, but we know all this, you've told us five zillion times! We love it, but we need to do whatever and go home! I want to save the animals like yesterday!" Mercedes was exhausted.

Alona Lois pulled out of the parking lot and as they were leaving the landing, lights began bobbing on the creek to the east and south and a boat with various people with colored hair (they could see in the truck lights) was slowly making its way upriver.

It appeared several people sat in the small canoe, and they were laughing and then slapping each other's arms.

"Get out of here," said Mercedes. "Those people are evil!"

"Yes, they are," said Malik.

"Bad witches!" said Alona Lois as she drove quickly from the landing and turned east on the two-lane paved road.

"At least they've left the house," said Malik, "as God planned it, for our protection."

He added, "We are one half mile from the house and the road to the right will say, *Lovely Lavender Lane*. Watch for it," said Malik.

They saw the simple sign, which read *Lovely Lavender Lane. Do not Enter.*, at the same time.

They all three said, "Let's go," at the same time and they felt the wave of cold chills but faith and the red Ford F-150 took the road like a pro, between ancient trees and around palmettos and scrub saplings and a few tupelo trees.

The driveway narrowed and wound around and around and into the yard of a three-story house which looked like it was from a ghost story. Which it was.

Mercedes said, "God be with us!" her mouth opened and her hand flew to it. She perspired at the hairline and Mercedes NEVER sweated stuff! She leaned forward in her seat and undid her seat belt. "Jesus Christ!"

The house had a Gothic roof line and at least three rooms, two on the right side, story two and one on the left side, story three, had pointed roofs. Every window in the house on all three floors appeared to be broken or missing.

Alona Lois said, "It's alright, just stay calm."

Malik, eased his truck door open and drew his gun and whispered, "Let's go!" He felt a burst of energy, although his bones hurt and his knees were knotty and so were both calves, but he at least had on Wellington boots to protect his legs.

Alona Lois got out of the driver's side door and said, "No, you go on," said Alona Lois. "Mercedes and I will come in behind you." She looked over at Mercedes who was coming around the tailgate and said, "Don't worry, I've got this!"

And it was at this point that someone flashed a light into their faces and yelled, "Stop, put your hands up, you are under arrest for trespassing!"

Chapter 8:
The Launch

Alona Lois stood beside the truck and was blanketed by the steep silence of the swamp and the spell binding dark night around Ebenezer Creek. She waited to see what was up next. She was a little afraid, but the truth is, not so much. Stuff just didn't scare her like it did a lot of women. She shaded her eyes from the spotlight and took note that neither her, Mercedes nor Malik had their hands up.

Who were these two men threatening them? They had not done anything wrong, well, you know, trespassing most likely!

Mercedes stood beside Alona Lois. She crossed her arms before her. They both listened hard.

Mercedes said, "We've done nothing wrong!"

"You are trespassing on property belonging to other people!" said U.S. Marshal Dimarks.

"I thought you were following Malik?" said Alona Lois. She raised the walking stick she carried before her like a battering ram.

Malik said, "I'm not your man. Nothing to do with a Fugitive list of any description!"

"You are the man who was camped out in the cabin on Big Daddy Island early this morning. We've followed you all the way to North Georgia," said U.S. Marshal, Dimarks.

Fancy meeting you guys here, is what Malik wanted to say, but did not. He said nothing but thought about the next step.

"They have to arrest us for something," said Mercedes and looked perplexed.

"This is a misunderstanding. This man is a friend, and he was staying in my yellow cottage with my permission!"

Alona Lois triggered Mercedes, who interjected, "That's right, her permission. We are just rambling around, la la la, God directed you might say."

"A misunderstanding, please," said Malik.

"So, you guys followed us up here, good grief, you've made a long trip for nothing! Talk about wasting gas," said Mercedes and laughed loudly.

"You do know you are on the site of a meeting place for a witch's coven. We are outside of Savannah, about halfway down Ebenezer Creek, where it connects to the Savannah River. This place has been staked out for months. You know where you are?"

"Yes, we know. God puts people where he wants or needs them to do a work!" Mercedes looked directly up at the eastern sky, when she said this, then at the U.S. Marshal in the eyes.

He did not blink but she didn't either.

It is a stand-off, thought Mercedes looking at Malik for an answer, then to Alona Lois who was interested in what Malik was doing. He was pressing the stones on the silver chain around his neck, and he suddenly had a tiny stone loose in his hand. He rubbed the stone, mumbling.

Malik handed the stone to Dimarks and said, "You dropped this."

"Thanks," said Dimarks, taking the stone.

"The fact remains," said the sawed-off Marshal, whose name was Force. "You folks are trespassing, and it could get dangerous before the night is over. We are busting this up and tonight is the night, I might as well say this, you must leave."

"Yes, thank you and we don't want to be arrested, but the fact remains we are God sent to save these animals in there." Mercedes said.

She stood there, arms crossed and waited for the man's response and rocking slightly on one foot.

"She is correct. This was my idea, not theirs but they are in this with me. We three are a team here," said Malik. "This is a mission for me. Something I've had planned for a very long time. We were going to Savannah and launch a mission from Tybee Island. But," and he giggled a little bit hoarsely, "we read these details on the cell phone you dropped and it immediately became God driven that we come here, you know twists in the plot, always!"

"No animals will be harmed in the writing of this story," Mercedes added.

The tallest agent wobbled and suddenly experienced a change of heart.

He spoke slowly and rubbed the jasper stone between his index finger and thumb. It was as though he felt a spell had been cast upon him or something! He staggered and steadied himself on his partner's shoulder.

He felt hypnotized by a spell. He backed away and dropped his light and said, "Ok, go do whatever you want." And the agents walked back to their SUV, hidden behind some kind of privacy fence. The car door slammed.

Alona Lois looked stunned but happy.

The only light now was the overhead, interior light of the Ford truck. In the dim light, Malik's flashlight cast a halo around her head and her eyes were wide as saucers at this change of heart in the agent. She whispered, "Well, I'll be..."

She stood there, across the wide yard from the Gothic house on the edge of Ebenezer Creek and felt awe that she was even here. She was a

Peggy Mercer

Senior Citizen, children raised, grandkids in college and one still in high school. She lived her life for them, as she had since the day her daughters and her son were born in these Georgia hills.

She had been the good mom and the devoted wife to Big Daddy, staying home, cooking and at long last, getting a very good job as a rural mail carrier when the girls had started school.

Her children always came first. One fur baby after another was part of their family life, because they love, love, loved animals of all stripes.

Right now, she had fields and yards with dogs and chickens, cats, and birds. In the field with a shed for shelter were two donkeys, more pets than anything else. Those animals were her heart!

Inside, at the house was a black poodle who was like her child, king of everything! Her constant companion...not alone even on this trip as the youngest grandson was there with him until she returned.

Alona Lois trusted the man, Malik. This almost never happened but once in a blue moon you meet someone you feel like you've known all your life. Maybe age was doing this to her, she did not know and didn't have time to figure it out.

Maybe loneliness and a drive for adventure had taken hold of her in the older years? She almost smiled. Be careful what you pray for, because the truth is she prayed for a greater purpose in life. And here it was. God himself had handed her a large adventure, out of nowhere.

Alona Lois smiled. She had to make sure they got the animals from that evil place before her, and she would. She was all business, and she would not stop until the purpose was fulfilled.

Plus, she blinked her eyes rapidly, little Mercedes here was her same age and they were the best of friends, laid in stone. She must make sure Mercedes didn't get hurt. Mercedes had not had an easy life and she didn't want Mercedes harmed.

Which made her think of the stone Malik had handed to the U.S. Marshal which laid a spell on him. Now that was interesting!

Alona Lois was ready, although her pulse was beating rapidly and truth, she had never ever even thought about robbing anyone of their animals but if she thought an animal or a child was in danger, count her in. Not her first rodeo. She relaxed and reminded herself to trust in the process and trust in the Lord for protection. She too, pressed the jade stone in the silver setting around her neck. Maybe, as Mercedes had often insisted, there was something to these rocks after all.

Alona Lois had been all over this historic area when the grandson had done research for the report which won him an award. Alona Lois remembered the macabre history when the Union Army had built the bridge across Ebenezer Creek, then pulled it up and let the freed slaves who were following them for protection, die horrible deaths in the swamp.

She didn't like being near the place where it happened, and she thought she heard weeping from the night shadows. Oh sad!

Only thing I know, thought Alona Lois, I'm like Big Daddy used to be, I don't pick a fight but if one breaks out, I will finish it! Especially if it involved people and animals I love!

Let's get this show on the road!

Alona Lois crossed her arms and arched her brows. She was frustrated, eager. Ready.

Mercedes said, "I knew it would work out. God always works it out to do what we are foreordained to do. He never fails me! Us!"

She stood still next to Alona Lois, who was taller than her but who always had her back. And she had Alona Lois's! Their friendship was its own beautiful story, and they were devoted to each other. More like blood sisters!

She felt confident in Alona Lois's no funny stuff, no beating around the bush attitude, all business.

Alona Lois was always honest with her even if the truth was a bit edgy or scary. Or not what she wanted to hear sometimes.

A best friend will tell you the truth, not sugar coat things just to make you happy. Alona Lois was a friend for the ages, and they often said like the song by Kenny Rogers, "You can't make old friends" and while it was true, they were older, they both had young energy and attitudes. And boy howdy, did they come up with some great events and adventures.

They had planned out and held with great success, despite some scary moments, a retreat for hurting women. With them, five women attended, three they'd never met before.

And angel had shown up, taught lessons and

then saved them from a boat which capsized off Sapelo Island. An angel, I kid you not.

Sopping wet, the ladies had washed up on the white sandy shore of a beautiful Georgia barrier Island. Uninhabited, if you remember.

The rest of the story is a story for the ages, beautiful, God-sent and God ordained. The women had been able to rise above their anger, their pain and find spiritual strength they never realized was within them. It worked when you trusted in God, which Mercedes did, above all.

One reason she trusted Malik was that she knew from the minute she laid eyes on him, he was God-sent for a purpose at which, that minute, she did not know the exact purpose.

She didn't fully know, but she knew partly and as she felt the presence of God, she felt trust in the presence of Malik. Mercedes was an author and thought, this is a great story I will someday write. She was like, on location, and she loved it.

But first, they had to live out the rest of the story, whatever it was to be. She was ready although she did sense danger.

It was darker than an oil slick on cement, but Mercedes felt comforted because Alona Lois was right next to her, and Malik was closer than a bond formed by memories of the past. And no, she could not "go figure" this out, not yet. No time.

Everything was about to pop, and she was hot as hades and her and Alona Lois were pushing up their long black sleeves.

The camo jeans were sticking to her thighs and Mercedes was thankful they had the good sense to wear wader boots. This was a swamp ya know.

The only thing I know is that this show must get on the road. This place is too dark, and we have a creek right off the porch there and we don't want to fall into it. She shuddered.

She felt special and this had been a fact of her life since she was born. Her granddaddy, an old timey preacher man had prayed over her many times those first years, to live and be healed. And she was healed of heart trouble and other ailments, and she lived and dreamed big. How could you not dream big when the one old man with the white hair you loved beyond life, talked about owning cattle on a thousand hills to adoring children who believed every word he said. Because he spoke the truth.

Mercedes smiled and prayed, "Come soon Jesus, and help us"! She mumbled in Hebrew.

As Malik stood slightly before the ladies, he thought, Foreordained, yes. I was born to do this, I am not and never have been, afraid of anything. I do things. I am a man of action and always was. Even when it hurts me and others, which I worry about even to this day. I never meant, nor do I mean, to harm anyone.

Even when I had the guy in a chokehold. He smiled. He had won more than a few arm-wrestling matches, in quiet places, on tables in bars, just like in the movies.

I am a perfect man of God. Not a perfect man, although God is perfect, but I am a perfect disciple and I have always served God above and beyond. I've been there through times, events, experiences, and if I say, here I am Lord, I have meant it before many times and I mean it now.

You sent me to do something, and I will do it. I may crawl. I may walk or run. I may fight my way in and fight my way out. But this mission is my heart and I know it's yours.

Malik thought of this mission in his final chapter of earthly life, to be the most important one of all. At least the most important right now.

He had always loved animals of all shapes, kinds, and stripes. He loved dogs, cats, monkeys, parrots, cows, hogs, and wild animals which he

found he could calm down, or "tame" almost instantly. Not sure if he was a horse whisperer but he was a whisperer to every animal he met, convinced the love of God, within him,
was known right off the bat to the animals.

Animals trusted him. Their spirit and his spirit bonded when no one else seemed to have that gift.

Many are the gentle, sweet, loving voices in my time on this earth when I have heard them call me the name Father and what an honor and a joy this has been.

Your love, through me, knows no end.

Your love through me, knows no bounds. Only the Glory bondage of which we know is the true vine running through our lives. The saving bloodline, the hem of your garment, Lord. I hang on and I do as I am foreordained.

Malik made the sign of the cross across his chest and moved forward with ease. He was old sure, but not out to pasture yet! He moved with purpose.

The night at Ebenezer Creek at the strange house on *Lovely Lavender Lane,* could not get any darker. It was creepy dark. The noises could not get louder, crickets rubbing their wings making songs, frogs croaking, the alligator down creek bellowing loudly looking for a mate.

Alona Lois smelled mud and decaying debris and sniffled, allergic to something. Mercedes sniffled and said she smelled a wet dog. Malik smelled victory and heard angels in Heaven warming up their instruments.

Malik hoped his knees held steady and his gun, if he needed to fire it, would not stick as it had a time before.

The house was three stories high and made from wide pine boards and poplar trees, which had likely been on the property. The yards were wide and overgrown, and the porch was a wraparound style which went all the way around the house. Malik shined a flashlight up and around about. They saw a back side porch that extended out and over the creek. It was made of wide wooden planks, cypress wood, and a rail ran around the entirety.

Pretty amazing place to be full of such evil, thought Malik. True Gothic in design, perfect for the devil worship inside. About to be imperfect!

He said to Alona Lois, "We will go through the front door, you both stay behind me. If shooting Starts, run. Drag Mercedes with you!"

As they stepped up on the front porch, seven steps in all, and stood before the door, Mercedes was chilled by the moons and stars painted on the door. Also, a color like blood.

"Is that blood?" she asked.

"No, it's tang," said Alona Lois, not trying to be funny but it did come out funny. Alona Lois did not laugh. Nor did Mercedes. Nor Malik.

Because at this point, they were scared. They were worried about animals trapped inside this mental asylum for evil people practicing some bad witchcraft! They had to save the animals!

The animals, no doubt about it, were to be used for blood sacrifices and friends this place was not far from Savannah, Georgia!

God-forsaken place, old house full of demonic practices, torture, and no telling what they did to the animals before they sacrificed them!

Malik felt a warmth about him. The stones warmed him. He wore 12 stones on a silver chain around his neck. The chain was a chain-link jewelry and heavy and solid. The stones were soldered on and wouldn't come off (unless he needed one to come off, then amazingly he simply slipped one from the chain!).

He didn't dare smile, but his heart was smiling. It was time for action. The mission of his heart and soul was here. The door will open, the thought.

For God plans our steps and orders them. And although this was a surprising twist to my earthly plans, God's plans are already in place and while I might not be aware of them, they are to be fulfilled just as I am. Amazing Grace.

God operates by amazing foreordination and amazing grace and mercy. His mercies allow us to live our purpose driven existence, and as we age, more or likely the repurpose driven older lives.

The angel in Heaven who is the keeper of the book of Names, wrote Malikhan Sharon's name down in the book a long time ago. Malik knew it. Over the millennial miles of his earthly journey, marks had been added by Malik's name, every time Mailk bore witness to history, prophecy, and the shaping of the spiritual world within which he was gifted to walk through.

Malik had become a man for all seasons but not like Jesus, who walked on water. Malik had been along for many rides, and his front row seat to the marking of the space beside his name in God's book, emboldened him to the next mission.

Now here he was for the two-mile final. Like an airplane running wide open for the two miles before lift-off, this was take-off time for this final mission. The rescue of precious animals.

Beulah Land, I'm longing to go there, he thought. In the glow of his flashlight, standing before the sun, moon, and stars door, smeared with dried blood, Malik could see something forming on his big hands. Specks of gold dust!

He turned back and shone the light at Alona Lois's hands. At Mercedes's hands. Gold dust!

Boy, they were in the circle you can count on it. Gold specks are reserved for special people in times of messaging from beyond the veil.

Time to launch the mission.

He was the Traveler.

The man with wings.

Worlds without end.

Chapter 9:
Malik's Mission

Malik placed his right hand on the doorknob, big and cold as ice, and turned it. Or tried to. It didn't turn.

Alona Lois was so close to his back he could hear her breathing. Mercedes leaned against Alona Lois. This was it. Open the door!

The three crouched, touching, two guns drawn and last in line, Mercedes pushing. She felt they needed to power through the door if necessary. Easier said than done. It wouldn't open.

As Malik twisted the doorknob and rattled it, the unthinkable happened.

Peggy Mercer

The barn style, solid wood, heavy with metal hinges on it, door which was painted with moons, stars, skulls and crosses, and blood-smeared drawings—*Tang*--Alona Lois had said—fell inward and landed on the floor. It sounded like a tree crashing to hard earth. An early train—People get ready, there's the train! A roaring, dust-flying crash!

Malik fell forward with the door, and Alona Lois fell on top of his back, Mercedes landing on top of them. This was a pile on a mission!

Imagine these three (two wide shouldered, tall and a bit thick) and one sawed off and petite piling up on a fallen door in a Gothic house suspected as a meeting place for a witch coven.

Imagine the three of them moaning and groaning, like Senior Citizens do when they fall over their own two feet, or trip over a dust bunny.

They crawl around on the floor and try to unentangle themselves from the various limbs. Arms, legs, and clothing and old age gravity refuses to let go, as it may have several decades back there. We are talking 60's and 70's my friends. Rolling Stones, ACDC, Def Leopard, Jimi Hendrix. Woodstock. (Back when we had energy!) Falling today and falling back then are two different events. They can't get it on like they did back then!

I mean here they are in a pile on top of a wooden door, big as a bass boat, not knowing if a leg or arm is broken, but praying not. Aches and pains and wanting to call 911. But also, smart and on a mission vital to Malik's life and by way of association, now the ladies' lives.

"I've dropped my gun," said Alona Lois. "And I can't see my nose on my face!"

"I've broken my right toe," moaned Mercedes.

"Shhhh," said Malik rolling over, freed at last from the ladies' weight, "there are guard dogs."

They were still on the floor, Malik sitting up rubbing his knee, Alona Lois flicking on her cell phone flashlight and holding it up into the Room. Mercedes coughing from the dust storm the falling door birthed and on her all fours, bracing with both hands.

"What guard dogs?" asked Mercedes. Jesus!

"I don't see guard dogs," said Alona Lois, or any other dogs for the matter."

"I do," said Mercedes. "Dobies...and they are coming at us," and she ducked behind Alona Lois, who had a gun although she would never use it on an animal. Dobermans will rip you apart.

Malik was silent and grabbed the chain around his neck and drew three stones off and held them in his hand above his head.

The guard dogs, with silver spike collars and snarling, but not barking, came around the corner of a stage built up higher than the floor.

They stalked Malik, Alona Lois, and Mercedes silently but for light snarling and baring sharp teeth. The dogs were black as smut and big.

There were three dogs (one for each person, Mercedes thought) and they were muscled up, well fed. The collars sharp spikes appeared embedded into their thick necks. Painful, Mercedes bet. Good Lord, have mercy!

"Be still and know that I am God," commanded Malik. His eyes were closed, and he prayed! "I am still," said Mercedes, "and I know God very well, thanks!"

"Talking to the dogs," whispered Alona Lois.

"Ohhhhh," said Mercedes.

"Oh, is right," said Malik.

"Maybe we can help them," said Mercedes and Alona Lois and Malik briefly threw Mercedes a look saying Lord deliver this woman!

The three dogs stopped about four feet from them and stopped snarling. They didn't move a muscle and watched Malik's big hands holding the stones and their heads swayed back and forth as he swayed his hand.

Even a guard dog likes to play fetch.

Malik threw the stones through the front door, jumped up and lunged for the door, grabbed one side, and with Alona Lois and Mercedes pushing, they raised the door and blocked the entry.

Malik propped a large metal bar standing beside the door frame, against the door on hinges. Nothing could break through it.

Malik was covered in sweat, arms, forehead, neck. The sleeves of his blue Polo shirt and the underarms were soaked. The front stuck to his chest. His tan arms gleamed with sweat.

He blew a stream of air, and took deep breaths and steadied himself, leaning against the door.

"Are you alright?" asked Alona Lois, holding her walking cane steady. She carried the thing to ward off danger, but now she steadied her aching legs which one felt broke at the hip!

"I am always ok, old but not done for," said Malik, and stood steady and backed away from the door. "Now let's find the animals we came to rescue!" So far, they had heard no animal sounds except from the Dobies.

"I don't see them, or hear anything at all," said Mercedes, limping on one foot. She stepped several feet into the room, then drew back and went, "Ohhhh Myyyy goodness!" She was shining her cell phone flashlight into the center of the cavernous room.

A circle in yellow had been drawn in the middle of the room and x's place for people to stand on. There were 12 spots. 12 witches, she realized. In the center of the circle, was a big splotch of rusty looking dried blood. *Tang*, as Alona Lois had said, trying to make it less horrible than it was.

But there it was, proof that blood sacrifices had taken place.

Alona Lois said, "Oh goodness," and stepped back. "I wonder if that blood has been tested."

"Blood on the floor," said U.S. Marshal, Dimarks who walked into the room from a back door, followed by Agent Force. Both agents had their guns drawn. "And yes, it was tested. Sadly, some of it is human."

"Good grief, witches!" gasped Alona Lois. She held her hands over her heart. The walking stick stuck out like a shield.

"We knew this, now we have to find the fur babies," said Mercedes. "Can y'all help us?"

"Yes sir, we'd like your help please!" said Malik. And Mercedes sure hoped Malik had more of the stone he had fed Dimarks in the yard a while ago. They may need to feed him more of whatever.

And Dimarks, said, "Sure, let's do what you have come here to do, so you can leave and let us stalk the house until they show up. By that time the local Sheriff and authorities will be here. You must hurry! Y'all can't be here when this goes down!"

He acted like a student on a field trip. Mercedes knew it her heart what was working the man. As it had worked the dogs. Malik's stones.

There was no time to quiz Malik about stones, although she was fascinated as it was pitch dark at this horrifying midnight.

She noted Malik had eased the stones on the silver chain back inside his shirt. Secret weapons.

Dimarks said a funny thing, "You have the stones?" and Malik smiled and nodded.

"Yes, I do."

They found the animals in wire cages and kennels in the room behind the stage. The scene was heart-breaking! Mercedes cried, and Alona whispered to her, "No time for tears, let's get these babies and go!" The poor animals wagged their tails although their mouths were taped, and they couldn't bark.

Malik carried a cage, which contained five tiny Yorkies outside to the truck. The yorkies' horrified eyes and their pitiful moans were enough to make a grown man puke.

"Take the tape off," said Malik," and give the dogs some water first, then grain feed." (Which they had brought in a sack.)

The U.S. Marshal, Force, said, "If you take the tape off, they will bark and draw attention."

"No, they won't." And Malik took a stone from the chain and rubbed each Yorkie on the head, and they became drowsy. They started trying to open their mouths with great effort, sore, and shy tails wagging. "Who did this?" said Alona Lois.

Mercedes opened the kennel door and put three babies in another cage in the back of the truck and as she did, she unwrapped and twisted off (gently) the tape on their mouths. All free now.

Unbelievably, on the pets' collars were the names and phone numbers of owners. The dogs had been stolen by the Witches Coven to be used for blood sacrifices. Demonic, bad witches!

Their toenails had been painted so Malik suspected a dog fighting ring as well. He and Dimarks talked about this as they walked back to the house. A lot more goes on in Witches' Covens than people can imagine.

Mercedes and Alona Lois gave the starving pets, water, and grain feed. They closed the kennel doors and the pets, never barking once, laid down to rest. "They knew." Precious babies.

Mercedes and Alona Lois both thought at the same time and said it, "They know." Animals are thinking, feeling intuitive and their spirits lead them, tells them what they need to know, guides them. No doubt.

Mercedes and Alona Lois, were caught in the middle of a rescue they'd never dreamed of, felt their hearts beating fast, sweating like Sea Biscuit (Mercedes) and Moving Colors (Alona Lois). Once, they had compared themselves to racehorses! Now they raced back into the house behind the men, staying close to Malik.

Going from room to room, they found four more cages, two were empty which they left behind and two held small dogs. One dog was a Pomeranian with gauze tape over this mouth, which he'd eaten through and was sick, so weak he could barely stand. Mercedes reached into the cage and lifted him up and out, wrapped him in her shawl and ran to the truck for water and food.

The other tiny dog was a white poodle, jumping up and down when Alona Lois took him out of the cage and carrying him in her arms, ran out the back door to the truck. Malik was standing there and rubbed a stone over the poodle's head and into its matted fur and the dog calmed down.

Alona Lois took the tape off the poodle's mouth and fed it water from a bowl, which she finally had to take away. She gave the poodle a few grains of food, then slipped it into a kennel where it laid down to rest.

"I am sick," said Alona Lois in a low voice, "And we need to go. I don't see anymore."

"The guard dogs. Dimarks and Force put them into a big kennel in their SUV and are taking them."

"Good grief, I'm sick too!" gulped Mercedes and hopped off the tail gate and leaned into the palmetto bushes. Alona Lois grabbed her waist and held her while she gagged. Mercedes bawled and gagged, bawled, and gagged. Which made Alona Lois bawl. Which brought tears in streams down Malik's face.

The night was darker than the bottom of a well and the silence thicker than milk clabber. Mercedes never threw up, but she wanted to. Her pain and disbelief had opened a flood gate of memories of her own beloved pets. Pets, who had passed away or ended in horrible deaths. Pets she loved like they were her children, still grieved!

She usually remembered them with Joy and Rejoicing but tonight, it was terrible pain. To see these beautiful pets locked in cages waiting to be slaughtered by demons was more than Mercedes could bear. It was sickening. Unbelievable.

Mercedes nor Alona Lois were dummies and they knew because they had read about it, and knew a few good witch types, but they knew there were bad witches who did stuff like this and worse. Child-trafficking, animal sacrifice, human torture. Sports among the elites of the earth!

They knew women who followed the moon and the sun and stars and did nothing but good deeds and helped people. The fact of people believing in spells and omens didn't affect Mercedes one way or the other. "Judge not" applied.

She had seen bad and this, at the Gothic house on *Lovely Lavender Lane* near Ebenezer Creek was the worst! This was not a play game. It was the sordid underneath of humanity. The cruel horror! How could anyone hurt an innocent child, or animal?

Mercedes could not stomach this evil stuff. She knew the world was full of it, but this insanity must stop! Mercedes never dreamed of such ugliness.

Whoever heard of a real Witches Coven so close to home? Practically next door!

Harming, no, *killing* precious animals for sacrifices? People needed to turn the evil ones into law enforcement!

She was thankful to Malik whose mission this was and who, by a twist of fate, had brought her and Alona Lois along to help. She and Alona Lois had done some crazy things but never like this. Nowhere near this dangerous.

Saving these pets was the crowning triumph, the elite victory of hers and Alona Lois's lives. She knew this and she knew that Alona Lois loved animals as much as she did, so, she felt the same.

They felt as Malik felt that animals are God's creations like humans, trees, earth, and God wanted them protected and loved. Animals love their families unconditionally, in many ways unlike people. Animals never divorced you! They never dumped you on a highway or in the woods and walked off and never came back. Would never betray you. Then sings my soul, animals to thee!

Animals refuse to leave when life gets rough. They won't leave you in sickness, and some won't leave your grave! Yes, we have guardian angels, and their names are **Ruffy, Rocket, Daisy, Moonshine** and more…our fur-babies!

Alona Lois grabbed Mercedes's arm and Mercedes hopped down off the tailgate. Alona

Lois and Malik threw canvases over the large kennels and secured the tarps with bungee cords.

She wasn't going far. To a church down the highway toward Savannah where she had a Rescue waiting to take the precious animals to the Vet and contact the owners and or/find them good homes when ready. Rescues are so awesome!

Malik was exhausted and breathed deeply but wore a bright smile. He stood by the truck and put his arms around both ladies.

He said, "Now, we will go. We've done what we came to do. It is time. God is happy!"

"Amazing nobody showed up but us," said Alona Lois. "I'm glad this is over, and we can leave." She crawled into the truck. The seat felt good, although the truck was hot and buzzing with a few Georgia gold ball size mosquitos.

The air conditioner came on immediately and broke up the night's intense heat. Mercedes hopped into the front passenger seat and Malik crawled into the back seat. They were exhausted.

"Where were the witches?"

"Mercedes, honey, they don't always show up, God has a way of taking care of us, y'all know."

"I'm glad it's over," said Mercedes fanning herself with a paper Funeral home fan. She rambled, "I was thinking about my friend Barbara's little dog, Pedro! I'd like to see those mean people try and grab Pedro. Barbara says he will eat you up!" She laughed but nobody else did.

Alona Lois cranked the Ford F-150 and backed out until she could turn around. She used dim lights to get a mile out of the driveway called *Lovely Lavender Lane*, then took a right on the highway and cruised on.

The mission was over and now Malik started preaching and what he shared with them on the last miles north toward Augusta, Georgia, changed their lives forever and ever. Amen.

He told them the eternal answers to questions older than Mount Ararat, and deeper than seven seas, higher than stars, and brighter than the rising sun:

"Do animals go to Heaven?" and, "Will we ever see our beloved fur-babies again?"

Chapter 10
Stroll
Over Heaven

Alona Lois, Mercedes, and Malik left Ebenezer Creek during the last hours of the darkest night *Lovely Lavender Lane* had ever seen. The night was July 3rd, and on the Georgia east coast it was the night of a full Moon, known as the Buck Moon. (Antlers in full "burst" on male deer!)

There were some clouds, like gauze in the sky which fell like a curtain over the face of the moon and made it look like spiders crawling for cover.

The Traveler

They drove down *Lovely Lavender Lane*, carrying seven animals in kennels on pillows, and blankets. The tiny mouths were open and breathing for the first time in days. The babies were fed, and tiny tails began to wag for the animals knew God had sent a message. He had sent deliverance from evil. Their Father in Heaven, God, who created them and made their families to love them had released angels to save them.

Animals recognize angels before we do. If one visits your house at night, a pet will let you know. They will wake up, ears pointed and looking at the slit of light under the bedroom door…go out and you won't see anything or anyone. But they know angels, and don't worry, they'll alert you!

The bed of the red Ford F-150 was a happy place as the big tires crunched along, headed east, then north toward Augusta, Georgia.

The cab of the truck was more than happy. Elated is more like it. Rejoicing. Born again!

Mission accomplished. Now what? They all wondered and knew the others were thinking the same thing. They had been up all night and were exhausted and running on adrenaline.

Now the sun was coming up. Jesus is coming soon, thought Mercedes. I hope I'm awake!

Up early down on the coast at Big Daddy Island, the trip to North Georgia at dark and the rescue of the fur babies, was taking its toll on all three. Again, they were exhausted!

The church was about 15 miles down the road toward Savannah, Georgia, where they were to meet a rescue. The rescue would take the animals, call people if possible and return the animals to their owners. The church was well lit with lots of people standing around, checking cell phones, and

The Traveler

taking notes. At a big tent, two ladies were serving coffee and sausage biscuits.

Teenagers strolled around carrying dog carriers and leashes and dog food in sacks.

The traumatized yorkies were shy and afraid, which was understandable and the poodle and the Pomeranian, which had seemed sick, were staring and with a little wag to their tails. Several of the rescue workers picked up the dogs and held them close, soothed them and washed their faces with soft cloths.

One owner, who had already been called, as she lived up the road in Ringold, Georgia, fell out of an SUV, grabbed a small yorkie, and shouted, "I've found my Betty Lou, I've found my precious baby, Betty Lou"! She wept loudly and wailed and a few of the rescue workers cried and hugged the lady.

Alona Lois and Mercedes watched this change of hands by the rescue organization and a Deputy, from the nearby town of Evans, Georgia, spoke quietly with Malik.

Alona Lois and Mercedes stood beside Malik as cameras popped. They smiled and tried to look serious because rescuing fur babies is a tough business. Later, they would note the newspaper photo looked beat to death!

"I am so tired I could sleep for a month," said Mercedes.

"Well, the sun's coming up, let's grab some of their coffee and biscuits and get on the road. I'm ready to get to a bed!" Alona Lois said and walked toward the truck. A lady rushed over and handed her a bag of hot biscuits and three large strong coffees!

"Thank you for saving the animals!" she said and hugged Alona Lois, who was shedding tears.

"We had to. No choice. We're animal lovers!"

Mercedes said, "Yes. We love fur babies. She has two donkeys in a field, too."

The deputy and a lady with a "Press" tag signaled them and asked, "Who owns the house on *Lovely Lavender Lane* and are people living there? Is it true it is a witches coven stealing, and using animals for blood sacrifices?"

"Well yes and yes. We don't know who owns it," she trailed. "But there are no more animals inside. We got them, plus U.S. Marshals got the Doberman's." She raised her fist and shook it.

"The FBI will put the people in jail."

"If they can catch 'em!"

And as the sun rose over Ebenezer creek at the juncture of where it joined the Savannah River, the red Ford moved smoothly east, again, carrying Alona Lois and Mercedes, and the man Malik.

Now, the three were crying up a storm inside the truck. They had loaded up, back at the church, said goodbye to the rescuers and church folks and settled in for the trip "home" which meant Alona Lois's house. Alona Lois planned to deliver Malik to his condo if she could find it. She didn't dare take him to her house. Too many little rabbits with big ears.

Mercedes had her own "room" at Alona Lois's home and Alona Lois had a room at Mercedes's house in South Georgia, as it was meant to be. Best friends stick together. Pray together and sort of get wild together, like this crazy excursion.

And often, at the conclusion of a major project or as Malik kept calling it, his "mission", they all were crying. They "told you so" to one another and Malik preached a spiritual sermon to end all spiritual sermons.

Alona Lois and Mercedes felt amazed as Malik shared the stories of his life (lives) and times and his hopes for them and every animal who ever lived or might live on planet Earth.

He had sung in the choir when growing up in the area, where his parents were members, a Methodist Church (I could say any church or religion but that would not be the truth. It was Methodist.)

And he sang now. Nice voice, though somewhat hoarse.

"Amazing Grace, how sweet…" in a low voice. They could hear that he'd once had a beautiful voice and probably sang better than they ever could. Except for Malik singing hymns, all was quiet as they traveled toward Savannah.

But Alona Lois came to a fork in the road and being smart, of course she took it and big Red turned left, north.

Alona Lois had another plan up her sleeve.

She needed to say Hello to someone, and her spirit said, *and goodbye to someone.*

Mercedes tried to sleep a bit—she prided herself of being a cat napper—but right now she could not fall asleep if she was paid a million dollars.

The mission fresh in her mind, the tears and love for every fur baby she'd ever shared life with, and there were so many.

Growing up on a farm, there had been pet chickens, a cow, horses, a big mule and many cats and kittens and dogs. Her favorite was dogs, although right now she shared her home in South Georgia with 8 kittens and four adult cats.

Her little boy Rocket had been killed by a speeding driver recently and she was devastated and planned to pray her way through the grief, which is what we must do to rise above pain.

Alona Lois kept wiping at tears and realized she had to see to drive! A cataract in her right eye wasn't helping at all and she nearly rear ended a 90-year-old (appeared to be) using hand signals from a 1968 Cadillac Eldorado. You could barely see the white bun above the seat!

Alona Lois was thrilled the mission had gone well and the animals had been saved and turned over to rescue. She was more than astonished how she and Mercedes had fallen into the adventure with the stranger, Malik. Jumping into the fire was not Alona Lois's m.o. but it was this time.

"This sure beat sitting at McDonalds watching people come and go," she said to no one. Oh, my goodness, I can't believe what we just did.

Malik was preaching the gospel to the ladies or trying to. If they would LISTEN!

"Some people don't believe their pets, animals, creatures, go to Heaven but I say that they do," he told them. "I know they do and have always known this."

"I believe they do, surely," said Mercedes.

"Of course," said Alona Lois, "Why wouldn't they?"

"Some people don't believe THEY go to Heaven," said Mercedes.

"Now that's the gospel, right there," said Alona Lois. "I cannot believe otherwise."

"I know for a fact animals go to heaven," said Malik, and he began the explanation they would remember and share with others for the rest of their lives. In tears and truth. Hold fast your hearts!

"Remember Noah's Ark? Why he loaded the big boat with animals, instead of humans?"

"Animals are pure in heart and full of love," said Mercedes, "and sometimes humans are not, and they are sometimes, in my thinking, dumber than animals."

"True, in the spirit. Animals are always all spirit and all love," said Malik. And so, riding along in the red truck, Malik began to minister to the two ladies, because his mission over time, was ministry and because he was closing the mission and his purpose in life (or repurpose) which is our greatest calling of all. Purpose.

"Make thee an Ark of gopher wood," said God our Father to the man, Noah." And as we've read, and studied, the fashion of construction came from God, perfect directions. "And who was saved into the Ark? Eight people of Noah's family, and then animals of the earth. Clean animals of every kind, by sevens, male and female and unclean animals in pairs of two, male and female." God prepared for the animals to be saved. Ahead of humans.

"Things unseen. So much more to the story of the world than our eyes can see!"

"People tell the story of the Ark but don't pay attention to its significance," said Alona Lois.

"Have you thought about this, then think with me," said Malik. "Following the flood which killed all the people of the world, during the days of Noah's Ark, what did God show the world he had created so majestically?"

"The ark sat on the mountain of Ararat," Mercedes said, looking around the front seat.

"Yes, it was a mountain peak, might have been at Ararat, or nearby, but way up there," said Malik, "but what was the sign?"

"God sent a sign of a rainbow," said Alona Lois quietly. This man was preaching it!

"Yes, and more than just a picture of a rainbow in the sky, the rainbow bridge."

"Oh," said Mercedes. "Cool. How do you know?"

"Well, I am a tradesman," said Malik, "and one of my trades is bridge builder. You ladies must know that I built that bridge in the sky and like any rainbow, the rainbow is still there. You might not see it, clouds may cover it, but I built the bridge, when God put the rainbow in the sky!"

Silence in the truck.

The rainbow bridge; always there. That is what this man said. He built the Rainbow Bridge!

Alona Lois wondered if Malik was so spiritual as to think this, make it up, really lived back in those times and somehow helped God to build the rainbow bridge? Sounded unreal but she hoped it was real! WOW! She began to pray silently. She felt she was caught up in a dream. And she loved it.

Mercedes loved this story as a writer, she vowed, naturally and without blinking to write this story someday. Good Lord, what a great story. And it was true, she knew. God have mercy!

Think about it.

Not just a rainbow in the sky, but a rainbow *bridge* in the sky. Animals on the ark...and a bridge for them, and throughout time, to cross when they came to their own leave taking into eternal life. A way out of here, just like humans headed toward eternal life.

Humans have a door by which they leave, and it is the same door they come through when they are born. Bands of Angels carry us home.

Malik, in the back seat of the truck, closed his eyes and prayed a prayer. He said, "God, thank you for the rainbow bridge. I built it to last, didn't I? Our babies have a way to get up there!"

Mercedes wept. "I want to hold my beautiful boy, Rocket, again and the other fur babies I've loved in my life!" she sniffled. "I want to believe this lovely story and I want to know my precious angels have gone across the rainbow bridge you built. And I do know it. Now, I know!"

Mercedes was a devout Christian who believed in the power of prayer and the supernatural existence of a loving Father in Heaven, God, who created every living thing. She had shared her life with many pets and now she was old.

She wanted to see her pets again. She wanted to see and hug and get and give kisses to every fur baby in her life she'd said goodbye to and grieved over. The rainbow bridge story is true, she thought as she cried. I believe I will see them again. I could not live any longer if I didn't believe this. How sad to heart I would be.

To believe this story, Alona Lois knew she must believe Malik's story of being a journeyman through time. So, if she believed this, she needed to believe in him. In supernatural beings, angels, people from other worlds. And she did.

She loved the Rainbow Bridge story as she knew Mercedes did, and she prayed often over the years that her own past pets had reached Glory land and somehow, someway, a bridge was there. Could be! God, let this story be true, she prayed and felt tears, cooler than summer rain, flow down her cheeks. Jesus, is this real?

The rainbow bridge, OMG!!! They were thinking as Malik continued to pray.

"Throughout time, and my lives, I have seen many animals in Heaven and around the throne. Every creature, great and small, is created by our Father in Heaven and he loves his creations. He created every animal who walked this earth, and he created them because he loves them so much."

"I believe this," said Mercedes, wiping her eyes as the beautiful sunrise glowing like a halo on red dirt fields and green corn and peanuts growing and sugar cane widespread on the hills of Georgia.

"Did you ever see a horse, in Heaven, lions or sheep?" asked Mercedes.

They were nearing a small town on the outside of Augusta, Georgia and Alona Lois said, "I've got to stop for a moment. We can get out and walk around. I am almost at the condo where Malik is living, and my home is not far from here. I need to stretch my legs!"

See, without you readers knowing this, Alona Lois was hauling two silk Boston Ferns in resin pots painted to look metal. They were covered in paper in the bed of the Ford F-150 and probably ruined, since I've been driving them all over Georgia for four days.

"I've seen lambs and lions sleeping side by side and as for a horse, sure. God loves horses and always did. I was there when the Heavens rolled back and I, myself, beheld the white horse!"

Alona Lois pulled the truck into a narrow gravel road and followed a winding path through Bell View Cemetery.

There were no tombstones, just tall pines, and stately oaks. Lush grass covered the rolling hills and nestled in the grass, bronze markers.

Alona Lois parked and got out and Mercedes hopped out as did Malik. They stretched and rubbed their shoulders and tried to release the cricks from their knees and backs with more than a few moans.

Alona Lois reached into the back of the truck and grabbed a fern and handed it to Mercedes.

Malik took the ferns and began walking. Alona Lois walked behind him, wondering, how did he know where to go?

The grave of Big Daddy lies nestled into the red dirt of Bell View Cemetery. It is a beautiful grave, as befits a legendary man and the bronze marker has engraving with his name.

There are a pair of markers side by side. The marker of Big Daddy, who died too soon, a husband, father of three--two loving and kind daughters (nurses) and a son who died some years prior—had an engraving of a tractor.

The matching tombstone was marked *Alona Lois,* with a birthday but no death date.

The three stood there.

"Hello," said Alona Lois. "I've brought ferns." And to Mercedes and Malik, 'He loved ferns!"

Malik sat the ferns down on the grass and with tears in his eyes, he thanked his Heavenly Father for this last visit here along the gravel path beneath the pine trees.

He relaxed and said a silent farewell to the place of rest. He smiled and thought of the many graves and tombs, through time, he'd stood before.

Alona Lois and Mercedes sat the ferns on opposite sides of the markers.

Standing before the markers, silence of many dreams, Malik saw himself as a young man with a head full of dark hair, and Alona Lois in a blue prom gown, smiling like the queen she had always been, the queen of his heart. And of course, right next to her elbow, their best friend, Mercedes.

Tears filled his eyes as he turned and walked away toward the truck. He never looked back.

The pathway was marked with small rocks and pebbles. He picked one up and wondered if it might match one of the stones on the silver chain around his neck?

He reached up and unhooked the silver chain and put the chain holding the 12 gemstones –for the 12 tribes of Israel--into his pocket. He rubbed the stones as he walked.

Mailk's life on earth was over. His journey through time had taken him many miles and now, on this last mile home, well, he felt like running.

He was almost there.

This final mission had been foreordained by his own destiny. By his Father, God. Malik was sent to save the trapped pets on *Lovely Lavender Lane* 20 odd miles northwest of Savannah.

A truly great part of the mission had been running into Alona Lois and Mercedes, wow, what a surprise (not) and over the short mission Malik's heart rejoiced.

Oh, how precious the love of others can be! Oh, how precious are the foreordained, ordered steps from our Father, God. What amazing plans he has laid for us. The people in our lives, our partners, children, family are our real treasures.

No matter how old you are, how sick our bodies might be, there is healing and most often, one more mission! We are never too old to dream.

Stay with it. Malik heard God the Father saying, never give up. Heed the calling and answer the voice of our Father God. Even though, Malik, who had been young and enjoyed so many journeys and missions through his time on earth, He would always answer God's call on his life. We are born, he thought, to walk and talk and live in the Spirit. Separate from this world. Chosen.

He handled his missions well. He had been a witness to the history of Christ. Malik could almost hear the padding of small feet as he and other children raced in fun, along the cold stones of Jerusalem streets, chasing a boy named Jesus on game days.

The silence of lambs as they gathered in the synagogues. Quoting, prophesying, healing!

The Traveler

He had seen, standing on the shores of Gennesaret, a man who would become Savior to the world, walk on water.

He had walked with prophets and heard their blessings and prophecies for the world and all creatures great and small, amen.

And yes, he had seen and shared his journeys along the times, God's way, with animals and saw first-hand how much our Father in Heaven loves them all.

Every person, every creature is a work of God, large, small, black, white, Asian, it doesn't matter. An artist loves his work.

Alona Lois and Mercedes walked along and stopped to pick up a silver chain on the ground. It held 12 stones set in silver.

And when they looked up, Malikhan Sharon was not.

Alona Lois and Mercedes knew they would see Malik again and every sweet animal they had ever loved. The sweethearts that were like their own children, the ones who had passed peacefully and the ones that had gone to Glory due to other's meanness and cruelty. Oh, how they longed to see their precious babies again, love them, hold them!

They hummed a verse from Malik's favorite gospel song, written by Mountain Man Carl Trivette, in 1952, written for his wife, Marilee Rasnake Trivette:

I Want to Stroll Over Heaven with You

I want to stroll over Heaven
with you some glad day
When all our troubles and heartaches
are vanished away
Then we'll enjoy the beauty
where all things are new
I want to stroll over Heaven with you

www.strolloverheaven.com

EPILOGUE

Some people don't believe in God, but Alona Lois and Mercedes did. They sat down on the grass as though having a picnic, in the early hours of the morning. They were alone in the cemetery, surrounded by soft noises of crickets, a frog hopping into a stream and water gurgling from a nearby creek. It was so early that dew shone on the grass and Mercedes prayed they didn't disturb any of the resting spirits.

Alona Lois prayed she could survive the memories of today without sounding like she was lying to her grown daughters and grands. It was all uncanny and then some!

It seemed unreal, Mercedes thought. It had been a long day and they needed to talk about all that had transpired because it was sounding a lot like something she had made up, fiction, ya know?

Crying was easy for the women because exhaustion makes a lot of folks' sad. They were too tired to talk, just cry. Alona Lois laid her head on her knees and cried. Not loud though.

Mercedes was an easier crier than Alona Lois, and cried openly and loudly, as though being torn apart. She wailed! Good thing nobody was out there but the resting ones.

"You are boo-hooing now worse than at the old house where we rescued the fur-babies!" said Alona Lois. "Shhh!"

"I've done a lot, in my life with animals but I've never rescued from a bad situation like that. Poor babies!" said Mercedes. "But I was not scared!"

"I was. I was nervous from this morning on, interesting man!"

"I heard that, looked just like Big Daddy. I nearly fainted to start with!"

"You know it, handsome and seemed a lot older than Big Daddy when he left this world a few years back. Even acted like him."

"And he loved animals!"

"Like we do!"

"Very spiritual."

"Big Daddy was always spiritual. He was in touch with his inner self and loved to talk about God," said Alona Lois.

"Did you see the little Pom back there and the poodle, so tiny," asked Mercedes.

"I actually told the rescue that if they don't find the family of the poodle I'll go back and get him," said Alona Lois.

"And I told them I would come back for the little Pom," laughed Mercedes.

"You know I've always said I wanted to start an animal rescue," said Mercedes.

"Hard work," said Alona Lois. "But I've always wanted to start one as well."

"We could start on a small scale!"

"I'm not able, too old," said Alona Lois.

And they looked at each other. "Never too old," they both said at the same time.

"We must love the animals and raise our voices for them. Rescue!"

"I've already got 9 cats and can't do anything else right now. You know my little boy Rocket died a few weeks ago. It broke my heart, and I will never be the same."

"Like to of killed me when Duke got snake bit," said Alona Lois.

"I am still crying over Rocket. I will never be alright again. It's hard to bear when you lose one of your pets. I needed this today. I needed to hear from God on Rocket going to Heaven. God sent a message to us."

"We got something out of this, for real, blows my mind. Very spiritual," said Alona Lois and handed the silver chain to Mercedes, who shook the stones and counted them. 12. Jade, Jasper, Mother of Pearl, etc. She passed the necklace to Alona Lois. Her hands and Alona Lois's were covered in gold dust! How about that!

And in the words of Malik, this came from Mercedes as she sat on the grass next to Alona Lois, in the cemetery in the Georgia hills, near Big Daddy:

"In the garden of Eden, God brought the animals he had created to Adam, who named them (formed from the ground or earth, as it was) and Adam named every creature of the field and the fowl of the air. The animals were formed of clay just as we were. Every living thing, God loved, because he created it."

"God's covenant with Noah and the animals into the Ark…" Saying, it was good, "Saying it was all good!"

"He said that six times," said Alona Lois.

"Who, Malik?"

"No, God."

"From the book of Romans, God chose to reveal his spirit, power, via the animals. God lives in each fur-baby."

"The plans for Redemption, and every living creature will be there on the sweet day when we see Jesus. Lying around with each other, the lion, and the lamb."

"They cross the rainbow bridge, who knew, and wait for us, every living creature great and small…" said Mercedes as she wept.

And they fell silent and in the silence of the resting place, they heard what sounded like a horse riding by. And a final whisper floated on the wind and said, "Behold a white horse…"

And as they stood and walked toward the red Ford, they swore they heard hoofbeats from the Georgia blue skies.

The two spent the night in the truck, "just in case" anyone appeared and needed a ride.

They chatted briefly about how our pets are loved like children and take a piece of us with them, leaving us forever heartbroken.

They knew they would never see Malik again.

But they had in their possession a silver necklace of precious gemstones, and well, that is a future story.

Mercedes talked about time travel and how this is the only dimension scientists have never been able to unlock. How we can't go back in time because God doesn't want us to. Those we love are not behind us, they are before us…which is where we are headed! Our beloved pets are before us, where we are going.

There is no going back.

God wants us to move forward with our cherished memories. Keep moving.

We have our own bridges to cross some sweet day, Rainbow Bridges.

>For we are Travelers.
>
>We have wings.
>
>Worlds without end.

Author Bio

Peggy Mercer has written many books, but this is her favorite, so far.　She writes about Georgia, people, places and especially the coast and countryside where rural people live in country houses with wrap around porches and children ride horses in their dreams.

She was born in a wood house near the Satilla River and grew up around campfires on the sugar white sandbars.　She roamed woods and forests and loved animals, all sizes, colors, shapes, and personalities.　The music she heard was dogs barking in the Georgia river woods.　The stories she heard were from family, cousins, uncles, and friends and spiraled up like blue curly q's from campfires of oakwood.

Peggy Mercer

Her first novel, *Strangers in Eden*, was a romantic suspense novel published in New York, New York by Avon Books and sold to five foreign publishers. The book was set in the Okefenokee Swamp in South Georgia.

Her first two children's books were published by Handprint/Chronicle Books, New York, and illustrations for *There Come a Soldier*, were created by world class artist, Ron Mazellan.

Peggy was winner of the 2011, Georgia Author of the Year, for her award-winning book for children, titled *Peach When the Well Run Dry* published by Marimba Books, Just Us Books in East Orange, New Jersey. The book is still sold in Washington, D. C. by the elite Children's Defense Fund for underserved children.

In both 2021 and 2022, she was named a winner of the GIAYA Award in the categories of Literary Fiction and Southern Fiction.

She writes and records songs in Nashville, Tennessee with jazz great John Richards, heard in over 60 countries.

She produces a You Tube podcast entitled, "Writing for Love and (Maybe) Money" and invites everyone to subscribe for free.

She has helped aspiring writers and edited for tv personalities and others and has traveled nationally as a keynote speaker.

Links:
www.peggymercerworldwide.org
Author Central on Amazon.
www.twitter.com/PeggyMercerBMI
and
www.facebook.com/*PeggyMercerAuthor*.

Peggy Mercer

Peggy Mercer, Savannah, Ga., 2008, Children's Book Festival. Member of Society of Children's Book Writers and Illustrators.

Special thanks to each of you who encouraged my writing throughout the years, especially Tim Morris, John Richards, Allen Field, Rhonda Sylvester Meeks, Brenda Finch, Shirley Perry, Lynn Barrington Pack, Faye Hanserd, Frank Harrell, and Joy Ford and others too numerous to name.

Special thanks these last few weeks as I grieved the loss of my precious baby Rocket to the Moon shown on the next page. Without him I am lost but surviving on the love of friends. I know without doubt I will see Rocket again.

God created every living creature and that means us and our fur babies. Run free my little music loving rock star and I'll see you over yonder!

Peggy Mercer

Praise for Peggy Mercer Books:

"Big Daddy Island books are wonderful reads. The first one, Another Island, Another Moon, changed my life. I know this one is good! My advice to her, Keep writing what God tells you. Never stop!" –Lynn Barrington Pack, Madison, Georgia.

"Give me a Peggy Mercer book! I will read and enjoy and be inspired with my own music and writing. She's done so much for me..."
Faye Hanserd, aka "Little Gladys" Nashville, Tennessee.

"Peggy Mercer and I have been friends for years and I love her writing. It helps me on so many fronts. She deserves every award they hand out!"
--Rhonda Sylvester Meeks, Nurse, Vero Beach, Florida.

Peggy Mercer

"Peggy Mercer is an acclaimed motivator of many artistic genres. Her work in music production is known throughout Nashville and beyond. She has been honored for her work in mental health advocacy, as well as books for children and adults. But her writing of The Traveler, set in coastal Georgia, is where the real Peggy Mercer shines!" -- John & Linda Oemler, Arizona Desert.

"I have watched Peggy Mercer write for longer hours than people work in offices, watched her struggle over words and phrases to inspire others and help them. Her words are gold. Her writing has shining moments and to hear others describe her makes me proud to be a singer of her songs. Her books are bestsellers and award winners." John Richards Jazz, Nashville, Tennessee.

The Traveler

"Peggy has written award winning children's books as well as bestsellers for adults. She writes from her heart and if you want to "feel" when you read, Peggy's writing is the place to go." -- Donna Kay Frisby, Ocala, Florida.

"I love Peggy's songs and books!! She has a special way of writing that comes from the heart. You will absolutely love reading The Traveler!" Crystal Gayle

"We have worked with Peggy for a number of years, she brings honesty and charisma to any subject. She works professionally and straight forward, a gem to any project." Randy Rich -- Randy Matthews, Nashville Music Guide, Nashville, Tennessee

Peggy Mercer

The Traveler

Peggy Mercer

Made in the USA
Columbia, SC
23 September 2023